Angus s **a moment**

'Are *you* c   as well?'

'No,' Janet replied instantly. 'No. He's just a big brother to me.'

'Any other men in your life?'

'No, and I don't need the big brother routine from you either. One surrogate brother is all I can handle.'

'How about a friend, then? We always did get along well.'

'Yes, we did,' Janet agreed.

Their eyes held across the table and in that split second, something changed.

Lucy Clark began writing romance in her early teens and immediately knew she'd found her 'calling' in life. After working as a secretary in a busy teaching hospital, she turned her hand to writing medical romance. She currently lives in Adelaide, Australia, and has the desire to travel the world with her husband. Lucy largely credits her writing success to the support of her husband, family and friends.

Recent titles by the same author:

MOTHER TO BE
POTENTIAL HUSBAND
POTENTIAL DADDY
DELECTABLE DIAGNOSIS

PARTNERS
FOR LIFE

BY
LUCY CLARK

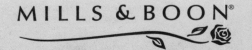

MILLS & BOON®

For my sisters—Kathy and Claire

First published in Great Britain 2000
Harlequin Mills & Boon Limited,
Eton House, 18-24 Paradise Road, Richmond, Surrey TW9 1SR

© Lucy Clark 2000

ISBN 0 263 82267 2

Set in Times Roman 10½ on 11½ pt.
03-0010-50355

Printed and bound in Spain
by Litografía Rosés, S.A., Barcelona

CHAPTER ONE

'HELP! Somebody, help!'

The call rang out across the restaurant and Janet's cup clattered instantly to the saucer as she sprang from her chair, ripping the split in her long skirt even higher.

Racing over to where the commotion was, she said firmly, 'I'm a doctor.'

'My husband is choking,' the woman cried hysterically. 'Help him! Please, help him.'

Janet hauled the man out of his chair and wrapped her arms around the upper part of his abdomen. Clasping her hands into a fist, she suddenly and firmly forced them upwards into the gap between the lower ribs, hoping the compression of air in the chest would expel the bolus of food.

It didn't. The man continued to gasp for air. The woman continued to cry hysterically. Janet tried to block out the noise, concentrating on the task at hand.

'It's all right,' she tried to soothe the man. 'Try to focus and relax your body. Relax,' she repeated, before urging him to the ground. She kept his head low as she struck him firmly between the shoulder blades with the heel of her hand.

Nothing!

A crowd was beginning to gather. The *maître d'* was hovering about, not sure what was happening but trying to calm the patrons nevertheless. The man's wife was now beside herself with hysteria and was sobbing frantically on another man's shoulder.

Janet grabbed the arm of the *maître d'*. 'Get me a vacuum cleaner and a bucket and then call for an ambulance.'

'A vacuum cleaner?' The *maître d'* looked at her in disbelief.

'Hurry,' she ordered impatiently, sending him scurrying away. While she was waiting, Janet tipped the man's head back and carefully tried to blow air past the obstruction. Every second he was without oxygen was bad news.

'Give me that,' a deep, male voice said briskly. Janet briefly looked up to see what was happening. 'Plug it in,' the man demanded, and then the vacuum cleaner was being placed on the floor beside her.

Janet resumed her efforts of expired air resuscitation, thankful that someone else in this restaurant obviously knew what they were doing and was going to help her out.

'Suction is ready. Sit him upright,' he instructed.

Janet lifted the patient to a sitting position and then looked directly across into Angus O'Donnell's hypnotic blue eyes, her stomach doing a little flip. So he had finally decided to show up—and about time, too!

Although, she reasoned, now was not the time for her to be mad at him. They needed to concentrate on their patient.

Angus placed the vacuum-cleaner pipe into the man's mouth, ensuring that the tongue was depressed. The patient started gagging as the suction began. Janet supported his weight, as well as delivering a few more firm blows between his shoulder blades.

Within seconds the blockage was cleared and Angus removed the pipe.

'Bucket,' Janet called and held out her hand, her eyes still watching their patient. She was handed the bucket and placed it in front of the patient who was now starting to retch. When he was finished, Janet ordered the *maître d'* to make him comfortable until the ambulance arrived.

'Thank you.' The man's wife grabbed her and cried into her shoulder. 'Thank you so much for saving my husband's

life.' Then she launched herself into Angus's arms and
clung to him.

'Go with your husband,' Angus told her gently as he all
but peeled her off him. 'He'll be fine but he needs you by
his side.'

'Thank you,' she repeated as one of the waiters led her
away.

There seemed to be waiters everywhere, cleaning up and
setting things to rights. The *maître d'* came over and stood
between Janet and Angus.

'Thank you,' he said in a loud voice. Most of the patrons
were settling back down into their seats, a hum of discussion in the air. Everyone became quiet as the *maître d'*
spoke.

'We would like you to know that our guest is now quite
well and recovering nicely. An ambulance is on its way but
the thanks go to these fine doctors here. It was fortunate
that they were dining with us tonight.' He turned to Angus
and shook his hand. 'This establishment owes you a great
debt and your meal with us tonight will be complimentary.'

The people around them started clapping. It was an an-
nouncement made for diplomatic reasons, Janet could tell.
The fact that the *maître d'* seemed to think Angus, being
male, had been in charge of the situation riled her even
more.

He was the one coming to *her* for a job. *He* was the one
who had arrived late yet *he* was the one who was publicly
thanked and offered free food. It grated against every fibre
of her being and, pasting a smile in place, Janet gave the
maître d' a brisk nod and stalked out of the room to check
on the patient.

He was sitting on one chair, his feet up on another.

'How are you feeling?' Janet asked, and smiled down at
him. His wife was sitting beside him, clutching his hand.

'Tired,' the man whispered, raising a hand to his throat.

'I'm not surprised. Your throat will be a bit sore for the next few days. Try to speak as little as possible and eat only soft, mushy foods.' Janet reached for his wrist and took his pulse.

'Stable?' Angus asked behind her.

'Yes.' The wail of the ambulance siren could be heard. 'Here comes the cavalry.' She turned her attention back to her patient. 'The hospital staff will probably want you to stay in overnight but it's just for observation. You'll feel better after a good night's sleep.'

'Thank you,' he whispered. 'I can't thank you enough.'

'You can thank me by getting well and by not breathing in when you're eating,' Janet teased with a smile, and he managed a weak smile in return.

The paramedics were shown into the room and Janet and Angus related the particulars of the incident to them, as well as providing the clinic's phone number for future contact. Once the ambulance had departed, they returned to their table.

They received a round of applause as they walked back into the dining area and the *maître d'* once again came over and pumped Angus's hand heartily, reiterating his thanks. Janet had had enough and, shaking her head in disgust, sat down at the table, not bothering to wait for Angus.

She mumbled under her breath at the audacity of the male species. Times had changed, she granted that, but even in this day and age she occasionally came across a chauvinistic male who refused to be treated by a female doctor.

The look the *maître d'* had given her when she'd asked for the vacuum cleaner had questioned her sanity. Had he thought she'd planned on cleaning the place for him? Stupid man.

'Isn't that nice?' Angus said as he took his seat opposite her and reached for his menu. 'He made sure I understood that we wouldn't be paying for a thing, drinks included. If that's the case, why don't we splurge?'

Janet continued to mumble and Angus replaced his menu.

'Bee in your bonnet, Janet?'

She glared at him and he laughed. 'Relax. Don't let that guy get to you. Let's enjoy ourselves.'

'No,' Janet replied, knowing she was overreacting but unable to stop herself. 'This isn't going to work, Angus. I don't care whether you're an old family friend or not, it just isn't going to work.' She looked at him—dressed to kill in a dark navy suit and collarless shirt. Had he always been this handsome?

'Don't be silly. Of course it is. You need a locum for your busy little Charlestown practice and I need somewhere to locum. It's perfect. The fact that we've known each other for years only adds positive reinforcement to the decision. You're letting that *maître d'*s attitude get to you. Let it go. He's not worth worrying about.'

Angus picked up his menu again. 'Now, I want you to order big and make that *maître d'*s head ache when he sees the bill.' He gave her his winning smile and Janet felt herself begin to relax.

'You're right. I'm sorry. I know I overreact but it seems to be happening more often than not lately.' She looked at her own menu.

'Hamish mentioned something like that.'

'I thought he might have. With Leesa working so closely alongside him, I knew she'd be bound to confide my troubles to him.'

'Hamish has always been ''big brother'' to the three of us,' Angus mused. 'I have no say in the matter—he *is* my older brother but with you two girls he appointed himself surrogate brother and protector.'

'I can't say I mind all that much,' Janet added. 'But I know Leesa does.'

'Is she still carrying a torch for him?'

'You know about that?' Janet raised her eyebrows in amazement.

'Leesa's been infatuated with Hamish for a good ten years at least,' he stated matter-of-factly.

'Does Hamish know?'

'About her infatuation? Yes, he realised a few years ago but he'd never do anything to hurt her.'

'There are different degrees of hurt,' she countered.

Angus seemed to hesitate for a moment, before asking, 'Are *you* carrying a torch for Hamish as well?'

'No,' she replied instantly. 'No. He's just a big brother to me.'

'Any other men in your life?'

'No, and I don't need the big-brother routine from you either. One surrogate brother is all I can handle.'

'How about a friend, then? We always did get along well.'

'Yes, we did,' Janet agreed.

Their eyes held across the table and in that split second something changed. Her awareness of Angus grew stronger and more intense. She was sure he felt it, too. Those deep blue eyes could penetrate any soul, she reasoned, and right now they were focused on hers.

She lowered her eyes first and looked blindly at her menu, trying to understand exactly what had passed between them. Her breathing had increased and she parted her lips to softly exhale. The faint flutterings of butterflies in her stomach surprised her and Janet's mind told the rest of her body to start behaving.

Angus was her friend—a brother—yet the look he'd just given her had been far from brotherly. His eyes had held a spark of desire—recognising her as a woman—and that *definitely* hadn't been there the last time they'd met!

'So…' Her voice cracked and she quickly cleared her throat. 'So what are you going to order?' She looked up again to find his dark head bent as he, too, concentrated on the menu.

'Champagne to start off with. The most expensive they have,' he added in a stage whisper, and Janet laughed. His antics had broken the slightly strained mood but she knew it would still be there as an undercurrent in whatever type of relationship they were destined to have.

It was true that this meeting had been set up by Hamish so they could discuss Angus coming to work in her busy general practice for six months. The problem was that Janet was really looking for a partner. The workload had increased dramatically over the past twelve months and another doctor was definitely a necessity.

The problem with Angus was that for the past eight years he hadn't been able to stay in one place for more than six months at a stretch. If she offered him the locum position, would he up and leave her in six months' time?

The thought of Angus leaving made her feel sad. Ridiculous, she thought. He'd only been back in her life for less than half an hour but Janet knew she'd feel a sense of loss if he left.

The waiter came to take their order, forcing her to put her inner thoughts on hold while she concentrated on having a good evening and a delicious meal with an old family friend.

'How long has it been since you were in Newcastle last?' she asked as they enjoyed a prawn cocktail.

'Eight years,' he supplied.

'Eight years.' She nodded. 'Roaming the globe. Footloose and fancy-free.'

'I keep in contact with my family,' he said, almost defensively. 'Although I travel a lot, we always stay in touch.'

'I can understand that. Even though our parents are archaeologists who travel and become absorbed in their work, staying in touch is important. At least Leesa and I have had Hamish here to rely on during the past sixteen years.'

'You relied on me as well,' he pointed out.

'Before you went away, yes, but I was still in medical school when you left. Hamish helped me through my exams and to establish my practice.'

'I used to pick you up from school,' he prompted, and they both smiled at the memory.

'Once, Angus. You picked me up from school once but, let me tell you, it was gossiped about for months afterwards. I'll never forget it.' Janet shook her head, her eyes alive with the memory.

'I was waiting at the bus stop after school with all of my friends. Then this huge hunk of man, wearing black leathers, black helmet and dark glasses, rides up on a motorbike—'

'A Harley, thank you very much.'

'And stops in front of us swooning, teenage females. Then he casually tosses a helmet at me and says in a deep and sexy voice, "Wanna ride?"'

'You pretend to think about it for a second, before shrugging nonchalantly,' Angus recalled with a smile. 'You put the helmet and your school backpack on, then lift your leg, revealing a generous amount of thigh under that awful school uniform, and swing it over the bike. Meanwhile, all your friends are staring dumbfounded and open-mouthed at your good fortune.'

'I slowly and sensuously slip my arms around your waist, revelling in the touch of the leathers, my eyelids fluttering closed in mock ecstasy. I casually blow my friends a kiss as you rev the engine, drop the clutch and take off with a loud squeal, leaving a skid mark behind us.'

They smiled over the table and Angus reached across and squeezed her hand.

'It was a classic.'

'The best thing that happened during my final year of school,' Janet said. 'I remember we laughed about it when we arrived home. Poor Mum was horrified that I'd been on the back of that ''contraption'' of yours and scolded you for being so irresponsible.'

'I forgot that bit.' He laughed and released her hand. 'We were always good friends.'

'Yes, we were. I wasn't infatuated with you. You were just…Angus, the brother I never had. I always did, and still do, look up to Hamish but with you I could have fun and that was very important to me.'

'Me, too. So what do you say, Dr Stevenson?' he asked as he raised his champagne flute in the air. 'Let's have some more fun together by working in the same practice.'

Janet lifted her glass to meet his. 'There are still particulars to work out, but…' She hesitated for a fraction of a second and then decided why not? She clinked her glass with Angus's, as though sealing the deal.

They both drank from their glasses and for the first time in months Janet felt a huge weight lift from her shoulders.

'So, boss,' he said with a cheeky smile, 'when do I start?'

'Tomorrow,' Janet responded. 'I'm not sure what Hamish has told you but in the long term I'm looking for a male partner.'

'Whoa!' Angus held up his hand. 'Partner? I thought it was a six-month locum job you had on offer?'

The weight returned. So he *was* only planning to stick around for six months. Why did that suddenly depress her so much? Why should she care whether Angus stayed for six months or six years? He'd be helping her out of her

present situation and that was all that mattered. She'd
known he wouldn't stay longer than six months. That was
the way he'd operated for the past eight years. Six months
here. Six months there. It was his trade mark. He'd been
offered partnerships left, right and centre, Hamish had told
her, but Angus had turned all of them down.

Nevertheless, Janet realised she was disappointed.
Disappointed that she of all people couldn't persuade him
to stay longer. Put some roots down. Take responsibility.

She sighed. 'It *is* a locum position,' she confirmed, and
saw Angus relax. 'I said in the *long term* I was looking for
a male partner. I've had a few patients giving me the run-
around because I'm merely a female who's supposed to be
chained to the kitchen sink, having babies. I realise that it's
probably sexist to insist upon a male partner and locum in
this case, but the fact remains that some people prefer to
see female doctors and some prefer to see male.'

'Steady on there, Janet.' Angus raised his hands in mock
defence.

'It just gets me so mad sometimes,' Janet continued to
fume. 'The fact that I've spent years training to be a doctor
and setting up my own practice seems to count for nothing.
I suppose if one day I do get married and fall pregnant,
those patients will expect me to give up my life's work and
just stay at home with a baby. I'd go crazy.'

'Of course you would,' he agreed. 'Which is why you
won't let it happen. You're carrying way too much stress
by yourself, Janet. So much, in fact, that you've got steam
coming out of your ears,' Angus teased.

She glared at him for a moment, before relaxing. 'You
could always get me out of bad moods. I never knew
whether to thank you or hit you,' she joked.

'Hey, it's part of my natural charm.'

'Along with your modesty,' she quipped, and they

laughed. 'Down to business. It's the beginning of July now so I'll have the contract of employment drawn up until the end of December. Does that suit you?'

'Yes.'

'Are you sure you don't want to make it a twelve-month contract?'

'Nope. Six is fine.'

'I tried. I can't say that I won't try again, Angus. You're a good doctor and I'm sure you've picked up all sorts of different skills on your travels. I could learn a lot from you.'

The last sentence had come out sounding way too provocative and she knew Angus realised it.

Once more their gazes locked, the atmosphere between them suddenly turning intimate. The background noise of the restaurant seemed to disappear into oblivion. Only the two of them existed.

She felt his fingers close over her hand but this time it wasn't a friendly gesture. His thumb rubbed little circles sensually over her palm, sending spirals of heat coursing throughout her body. Her eyelids fluttered closed for a brief moment, her senses reeling at his touch. She breathed in deeply and realised she could smell cologne. Opening her eyes quickly, she found he'd moved and was now closer—within kissing distance.

'Shall we seal the deal?' he asked, his voice deep and husky, his eyes filled with desire. Janet knew her own green eyes would have mirrored the emotion.

She opened her mouth but no sound came out. Involuntarily, she licked her lips only moments before Angus pressed his own to hers in a mind-shattering kiss.

He tasted like champagne, sweet and bubbly and going straight to her head. Gently he wove his magic around her as he coaxed her lips apart, momentarily slipping his tongue between them.

Slowly he withdrew, leaving her shivering with anticipation and excitement. It was the very first time Angus had ever kissed her and Janet secretly hoped it wouldn't be the last.

'Get a grip,' Janet ordered her reflection. She'd quickly excused herself and rushed to the ladies' room as a means of escape. She pulled out her mobile phone and pressed the speed dial button for Leesa's mobile. Moments later, her sister answered.

'Leesa, it's me.'

'How's dinner going? Has Angus showed up?' Leesa asked with interest.

'Has he ever,' Janet mumbled, before clarifying, 'He was a little late but, considering there was an emergency, it didn't matter.'

'Oh? What emergency?'

'Leesa!' Janet protested. 'Can you stop thinking about medicine for one second? You're becoming more and more like Hamish every day.'

'I take that as a compliment.' Leesa laughed. 'You sound in a tizz. What's up, sis?'

'Angus—that's what.'

'What about him?'

'He… That is, I mean… We…just…' Janet trailed off, not at all sure how to tell her sister what had happened.

'Spit it out, Janet,' Leesa coaxed.

'He kissed me,' she blurted. There was silence on the other end of the phone.

'Where are you?'

'In the ladies' room. I needed to escape. He's waiting for me, Leesa, but I don't want to go back out there.'

'Why? Didn't you *like* the kiss?'

'Of course I liked the kiss,' Janet replied quickly. 'But this is *Angus*. I've known him for years and not once—not *once*—have I ever thought of him...*that* way before. He's always been a surrogate brother.'

'You're talking to the wrong person, darling. I've been in love with Hamish for so many years it's no longer funny. These O'Donnells have a strange knack of weaving their spells over the Stevenson women.'

'Will you cut it out? Tell me what I should do.'

'OK. In the past, you've always seen Angus as a brotherly figure. Correct?'

'Yes.'

'So how do you feel about him now? Still brotherly?'

'Of course,' Janet answered instantly.

'Yet you just allowed him to kiss you, and not five seconds ago you admitted that you liked his kiss.'

'What are you getting at?'

'You no longer look upon our darling Angus as just a brother any more.'

'Thank you, Dr Freud,' Janet quipped. 'Now what am I supposed to do? I'll be working closely with him at the surgery and, as everyone knows, Angus only stays for six months. That's it. No more, no less. I'd just be setting myself up for heartache if I allowed this...this spark of attraction between us to ignite into something more.'

'Correct,' Leesa confirmed. 'Take it from me. The last thing our family needs is yet another Stevenson woman pining for an O'Donnell she can't have. Leave that to me.'

'Why do you do this to yourself, Leesa?'

'Because I love Hamish,' her sister replied. 'It's as complicated and as simple as that. One day he'll see me for the woman I've become, not the little sister he's never had, but that's not the issue here. The question is, what are you going to do about Angus?'

'Pretend it didn't happen.'

'There you go. Decision reached. Hold on a second.'

There was muffled conversation in the distance then Leesa quickly returned her attention to her sister.

'Hamish has just told me they're ready for us in Theatre so I'd better go. I'll only be a few hours so call me when you get home and let me know how things went.'

'OK. Thanks, Leesa.'

Janet rang off. Pretend it didn't happen. Easier said than done but, nevertheless, that was her plan of action.

After checking her make-up and giving her shoulder-length, strawberry blonde hair a quick brush, Janet took a deep breath and returned to their table.

Their main courses had just arrived, so she was spared any embarrassment about the kiss she was desperately trying to forget.

Angus was an entertaining dinner companion. He related many anecdotes from his experiences overseas while they ate the scrumptious food.

'When I was in the Lake District, one of the other doctors in the practice was bent on playing practical jokes on everyone. The whole surgery buzzed with laughter and I swear the patients recovered so much faster because of the doctor's attitude. After being there for three months, it occurred to me that although he played a lot of jokes on everyone else no one seemed to play any on him.'

'And Angus O'Donnell decided to change all that?' Janet guessed.

'Correct. One Friday night after he'd been down at the pub for a drink and then some, he went back to his room above the surgery and went to bed. Out cold he was, as he always was when he wasn't on call on the weekends.

'I'd arranged for the receptionists to help me out and together we mixed up some plaster of Paris and put a cast on his leg while he slept.'

'He didn't wake up?' Janet asked incredulously.

'Didn't even stir,' Angus confirmed. 'The next morning he had football practice—'

'That's soccer, isn't it?'

'Yes. I was on call that weekend and heard the commotion when he woke up. It was hysterical. We took photographs of him almost falling down the stairs with this dead weight of plaster on his leg.'

'What was his reaction?'

'He loved it. The only thing that bothered him was that he hadn't thought of it himself.' Angus laughed. 'Do you know, he insisted on going out and getting all his football mates to sign his cast before we cut it off. Quite a card he was. A good sport as well.'

'If you liked it so much, why didn't you stay?'

'England's not my home,' Angus responded, his body language instantly defensive.

'But didn't they offer you a partnership?'

'The question you need to ask, Janet, is, who didn't offer me a partnership?' He leaned back in his chair, the look he gave her indicating she should back off. 'I'm just not interested in any permanency in my life at the moment.' The words were delivered with sterile formality.

'When will you be?' she asked quietly, not taking the hint. The jovial mood they'd shared had disappeared.

'Your guess is as good as mine.' He shrugged. 'For now, if you've had enough to eat at the restaurant's expense, I think we should head home. After all, I'm due to start a new job tomorrow.'

'Yes, you are,' Janet confirmed, allowing him to change the subject. Something strange had just happened. It was as though a piece of the puzzle was missing but she wasn't going to discover it tonight. 'I believe your new boss is a stickler for punctuality.'

'I have heard that rumour,' he agreed with a smile that didn't quite touch his eyes.

They stood and went over to the *maître d'* who once again thanked them profusely and wished them goodnight.

Out in the car park, Janet hesitated. What now? Did he walk her to her car and then kiss her again? Bid her a sweet farewell? Or did she just walk away, casually saying she'd see him tomorrow?

'Where's your car?' he asked, and she pointed to the cherry red Hyundai Excel Sprint. 'Then let's go.'

'Go? Go where?'

'To your place,' he said matter-of-factly.

'What do you mean?' she asked with a hint of panic.

'I'm moving in with you.'

CHAPTER TWO

'YOU are *not* moving in with me, Angus O'Donnell.' Janet clutched her hands to her chest, as though protecting her heart from him.

'Hamish told me that you had extra room now Leesa's moved to an apartment closer to the hospital.'

The panic started to subside and Janet breathed a sigh of relief. 'You mean the duplex.'

'Correct.' He gave her a puzzled frown, before saying with complete seriousness, 'You thought I wanted to move in and share a bedroom, didn't you? Shame on you,' he added before she could reply to his question. 'I thought we were friends. I'll have you know that I'm not that kind of man.'

Janet watched him closely and finally saw the twitching at the corners of his lips. She laughed. 'You almost had me.' She shook her head in disgust as he joined in the laughter. 'I should have remembered your quirky sense of humour. You knew I'd jump to the conclusion that…when you said… Ooh, you are the master teaser, Angus O'Donnell.'

'Thank you, thank you.' He took a bow.

'You do realise that now I'll have to retaliate.'

Angus leaned in closer and placed a kiss on the tip of her nose. 'I'm looking forward to it.' He raised his eyebrows suggestively, his smile almost wolfish. 'Now, let's take your shiny red car for a spin. Do I get to drive?'

'Where's your car?' she asked, but knew the answer before he said it. When a man spent only six months in one place, he didn't want to worry about buying and selling cars all the time.

'Hamish has arranged for me to lease a car while I'm here. I'm picking it up tomorrow. In the meantime…' He held out his hands for the keys. When she hesitated he teased, 'Come on, Janet. You've driven with me before.'

'Why do you think I hesitate?' she retorted, enjoying being with him. 'All right.' She gave in and handed the keys over. To her surprise, Angus unlocked her door and held it open for her. He'd never done that before. Perhaps all those foreign countries he'd worked in had improved his manners—slightly!

She gave him directions but as he'd grown up in Newcastle and its surrounding suburbs he remembered the area well.

'You've…changed, Janet' he remarked when they stopped at a red light. He turned to face her and their eyes held.

'I should hope so,' she replied as she nervously licked her lips. 'After all, it has been eight years.'

'Yes, but there's something else. Something different about you.' The magnetic pull they'd experienced a few times during dinner was once again evident.

The light turned green and he returned his attention to the road. The conversation was kept to general topics as Janet pointed out some of the developments as they drove down the main street of Newcastle.

'Turn right here and we'll go past the surgery. It's one of the lovely old houses from the nineteen twenties which I had renovated. They were going to tear it down so basically I got it for a bargain price even though the land cost was high.'

'You would have had to meet strict renovation standards, considering you were looking at practising medicine there. That alone would have added to the cost of everything.' He

stopped in front of it when she pointed out the building.
'You'd probably have done better leasing a few consulting
rooms in one of the office buildings in the main street.'

Janet took exception to his words. 'No, Angus. I
wouldn't have done better doing anything other than what
I *wanted* to do. This is *my* practice so I invested in what *I*
wanted to have. I've always wanted an old house renovated
into a surgery. It lends a more homey air to the atmosphere
and ultimately makes the patients feel as though they're not
just numbers, but people in their own right.'

'It was only a suggestion,' he offered with a shrug, and
put the car in motion again. 'I'm sure you've done the best
thing for you.' He turned left and drove the two blocks
from the surgery to where Janet had told him she lived.

'In other words, you know Hamish wouldn't have let me
get into anything over my head.'

'Exactly. Big brother Hamish has always been there for
all of us. He's not about to break a habit of over twenty
years. If I'd been here, I simply would have offered different advice.'

'Well, you *weren't* here, Angus.'

The tension in the car was becoming unbearable. 'Let's
drop the subject,' he said after a few minutes' silence. He
pulled the car into the driveway and waited while Janet
pulled a remote control from the middle console of the car.
She pressed the button and the garage door went up.

Angus drove in and cut the engine. Janet climbed out of
the car and unlocked a door that led into her house. She
quickly pressed the code for the house alarm to deactivate,
before walking through to the kitchen and switching the
kettle on.

Although they'd had coffee at the restaurant, after the
conversation in the car she definitely needed another cup.

How could he have been back in her life for less than
three hours and have made her feel such a multitude of

emotions? She'd never had this roller-coaster feeling with anyone else—not even the Angus she'd grown up with. Usually she was so easygoing but he seemed to be bringing out such different sides of her personality that it was starting to scare her.

The kettle whistled its tune and switched off. Janet automatically went through the motions of making coffee. She'd taken a sip before she realised Angus hadn't followed her in as she'd expected him to.

Replacing her cup on the bench, she retraced her steps to the garage. He wasn't there. The car was locked up and the garage door was closed. There was no sign of Angus.

Janet walked slowly back through her house to the front door. She went outside and across the small pathway that connected the two houses. She and Leesa had invested in this place when their parents had sold their family house.

They'd decided to sell as they were only in Newcastle for four weeks of the year, their work with universities and the digs they were on taking up the other forty-eight weeks.

That was how her parents had met the O'Donnells. Angus's parents were archaeologists as well and the two couples had started a company, employing many young and eager students on the several sites they excavated yearly.

Janet's mother had stayed home until Leesa had finished high school, but once she'd started medical school Carol Stevenson had declared that her daughters had been old enough to fend for themselves.

Janet knew her mother had peace of mind, knowing Hamish kept a close eye on her daughters. As he was nine years older than herself and eleven years older than Leesa, he had guided them both during their careers.

The door to Leesa's half of the duplex was open and two large boxes sat on the doorstep. Janet frowned and walked inside. She checked the alarm panel but found it deactivated.

'Angus?' she called, and waited.

'In the kitchen,' he called, and she walked through the house which had the reverse layout of her own. She found him unpacking his kettle and coffee-cups.

'What are you doing?'

'Moving in. What does it look like?'

'How did you get in?'

He held up her car keys. 'I figured one of these would open the door and it did. Only took me two tries. The first one must open your door.'

Janet marched over and took the keys from his hand. 'And the alarm?'

'Hamish gave me the code.'

'Where did these boxes come from? Did they just miraculously appear?'

'No. Hamish had them sent over earlier this evening.'

'So you knew they'd be here, waiting?'

'Yes.'

'All neatly planned, wasn't it—you moving in here? What if I'd said no? What if I'd had someone else who was planning to move in?'

'Do you?' he asked as he rinsed the kettle, before filling it with water.

'N-no,' she stammered. 'But that's beside the point.'

'Which is?'

'The fact that it's been decided that you would live here without even asking my permission first. You announce that you're staying here. Hamish organises for your stuff to be sent. You take my keys instead of asking for your own. You've barged your way not only into my home but into my practice as well.'

'Janet.' Angus crossed to her and placed his hands on her shoulders. 'I'm sorry.' His face reflected his apology. Janet looked for signs that he was teasing her again but found none.

'I'm sorry I assumed so much. Hamish told me about the job and the fact that Leesa had moved. It all seemed to fit. A job for six months, somewhere to live.'

'And a car ready by tomorrow,' Janet added. 'I don't *mind* so much that you're here, back in Newcastle, Angus, but I do mind being railroaded by the O'Donnell brothers. I know Hamish wouldn't have thought twice about what he was doing. You're his brother, I'm his ''sister''. Everything was logical. If I didn't love him so much I'd throttle him.

'What neither you nor he seem to realise is that the Stevenson girls have grown up. We *can* make our own decisions. We *can* make our own mistakes. If we require your *advice* we know we can ask for it and receive an honest opinion, but when you both just take over my life, the way you have tonight, it makes me feel manipulated.'

'Janet, no. That wasn't our intention.'

'I know,' she said and shrugged his hands off her shoulders. He was too close for comfort and she needed some space between them. 'It does work out well. I need a male doctor—you're back in town to help out. You needed somewhere to live and work—it's all here, falling right into your lap. As I said, that doesn't bother me. It does work out well for everyone concerned. All I'm *asking* is that next time you do just that—*ask*.'

'I'll try to and I'll speak to Hamish about it as well.'

'No.' Janet shook her head. 'I can speak to him myself, thank you. Now, would you like me to help you unpack and settle in?'

'Yeah.' He nodded and gave her that lopsided grin that made her heart race. 'On one condition.'

'What?' she asked cautiously.

'That you loan me some coffee.'

Janet laughed. 'Come next door and have a cup, then we'll get to work here. I'll also give you your own keys so you don't need to borrow mine again.'

Over coffee, they discussed the consulting hours and the type of patients who were currently on Janet's files.

'I hold a morning clinic on Saturdays and take Saturday afternoons and Sundays off, although any patient can call me after hours for a consult in an emergency.'

'But the hospital's only about twenty minutes away. Why can't the emergencies go there?'

Janet watched as he raised the cup to his lips and took a sip of the hot liquid. The walls of her kitchen seemed to be closing in on them as the atmosphere became more personal.

'B-because that's not the way I want it,' Janet stated. She needed to keep the conversation professional. After all, they were to be colleagues.

'Noted.' Angus nodded.

'The patients are mainly mid-forties upwards, although I do have a few young families.'

'And then there are your chauvinistic patients,' Angus added.

Janet shook her head in disgust. 'Mr Davies. He's booked in tomorrow—to see you.'

'Thanks for the welcome.' He laughed. 'Or is it initiation?'

'Something like that.' She looked at the clock. 'We'd better get you settled in. Fortunately for you, Leesa left a little bit of furniture behind. She couldn't fit it all into her apartment. So you have a bed and a few tables and chairs.'

'It's not a bed, Janet. It's a single mattress which is far too small for me but will nevertheless get me through the night. Tomorrow is leasing day.'

Together they unpacked his boxes. One box held clothes—which she let Angus unpack. It was personal enough, going through his other belongings. As she unpacked the second box, which contained crockery and linen, she gained a more intimate insight into the man he now was. Black satin sheets? She lifted the fabric and brushed it across her cheek, her heartbeat racing as her mind thought up a variety of images—all of them involving herself and Angus in hot and passionate clinches.

'Janet?' he called, and she dropped the sheet as though it were on fire. He walked into the spare room where she was putting the linen in the cupboard. He took one look at her face and the rumpled sheet on the floor. A small smile spread across his face and he raised an eyebrow, before leaning against the doorframe. 'Need any help?'

Janet quickly bent to pick up the sheet and stuffed it into the cupboard. 'Nope. All finished here.'

'Good.'

He was letting her off the hook, she could tell.

'Just one more box to go,' he said, stepping into the hallway. She followed him out and into his kitchen. 'It contains non-perishable foods, minus the coffee...' He smiled at her. 'And things I've picked up over the years. I'll do them later.'   ·

'So...that's it?' Janet asked. 'Your worldly possessions?'

'That's it. Believe me, at times it feels like a lot. I started off with one box.'

'You've graduated to three boxes in eight years? I'd say that's good going.'

'I guess so.' He shrugged. 'Thanks for your help. I'll let you get to bed now.'

He walked her to her front door, his hands shoved into his pockets.

'You'd better come over for breakfast,' she suggested. 'After seeing what we unpacked tonight, furniture and a car won't be all you're acquiring tomorrow.'

'Thanks.' He seemed genuinely touched. 'I'll do that. Around seven?'

'Sounds good. Angus...' Janet hesitated. 'I *am* glad you're back.'

'Me, too.' He bent his head and kissed her. Not once but twice. 'See you in the morning.'

At five to seven next morning, Janet started to fidget nervously about her appearance. Her hair was neatly braided and out of the way, and she was dressed in pressed linen trousers, navy in colour, a white shirt with embroidery around the collar and a cardigan. For the short walk to work, she'd put her thick woollen coat, gloves and scarf by the door.

At seven o'clock, she rechecked the food. The bread was ready to toast, the coffee was warm and inviting her to sneak a cup before Angus arrived. She resisted. There was orange, apple and pineapple juice in the fridge and some fresh fruit on the table.

The timer over the oven buzzed and Janet quickly took the fresh muffins out, breathing in their delicious scent as she did so. She rarely went to such trouble for herself, but having someone else to share the most important meal of the day with was cause for celebration.

At least, that was what she told herself. It was only because she'd become so used to eating breakfast alone that she'd gone to so much trouble this morning. Even when Leesa had been living next door, they'd rarely shared breakfast. As an orthopaedic registrar, Leesa was either working or sleeping when Janet was beginning her day.

She looked at the clock again as she transferred the muffins from the tin to the cooling rack. Then she quickly checked that the door was unlocked, all ready for her to call out casually for Angus to come in when he knocked.

At five past seven there was still no sign of him. Janet went into her bedroom and to the wall that connected the two houses. Pressing her ear to the plasterboard, she listened. Nothing!

Perhaps he was just running a little late. It didn't matter.

It just meant not having the luxury of eating a slow and healthy breakfast.

At ten past seven Janet had had enough. She grabbed her keys and marched over to Angus's house. She knocked quietly on the door but received no answer. She knocked harder—still no answer. She pounded on the door—nothing!

A multitude of scenarios flashed through her mind as her imagination went into overdrive. Was he OK? Had he hurt himself?

Janet pushed her key into the lock and opened the door. 'Angus?' she called out, but received no reply. She couldn't hear running water so that indicated he wasn't in the shower. She walked to the bedroom that had the mattress in it and quietly knocked on the door.

No answer.

Slowly she turned the handle and opened the door. Only then could she hear the heavy breathing of the man who was occupying more of her thoughts than she liked.

He looked so adorable, lying there with a blanket flung haphazardly around him, his head resting on a pile of jumpers in lieu of a pillow. His feet were hanging over the edge of the mattress and even though he was sleeping diagonally his arms were folded uncomfortably above his head. All this time she'd been working away, preparing a scrumptious breakfast for the two of them, and he'd been sleeping.

Anger and frustration welled up inside her and she said loudly, 'Angus. Wake up!'

He stirred and turned over, one leg flung out of the blanket. 'Janet?' he mumbled, and then a slow smile spread over his face. 'Janet,' he breathed huskily. 'Come here and join me.'

Janet could have sworn that in that split second her heart stopped beating. Join him? The words produced a barrage of imagery in her mind. Both of them naked on that tiny little mattress. It might be uncomfortable but, then, comfort was a relative thing in those situations.

'Stop,' she ordered her thoughts out loud. This was *Angus* —the guy she looked upon as her brother. She shook her head. The sooner she was honest with herself, the better. She was downright attracted to him. He was no brother of hers and she wouldn't mind him being something a lot more intimate than just a friend. *He* was the sole reason she'd gone to so much trouble this morning to provide a wonderful breakfast. To show him what a good cook she was.

And here he was—sleeping!

Janet walked over and shook his arm. 'Angus, wake up. It's almost a quarter past seven and we're going to be late.'

'What?' He slowly opened his eyes and squinted up at her. She walked over and yanked the curtains open, flooding the room with sunlight.

'Make sure you put an alarm clock on your long list of things to buy today.' She walked back to the door. 'Breakfast is getting cold. You have ten minutes before I throw the fresh, home-baked muffins in the bin.'

'What?' he mumbled again as he rubbed his eyes. He looked so incredible that Janet was tempted once again to go with his first offer, and join him. Instead, she decided to use the attraction to her advantage and get him out of that bed and ready for work.

'You *do* remember what a good cook I am, don't you?' she asked provocatively, and swished her hips.

'How could I forget?' He was awake now and gave her a brilliant smile.

She hesitated very fleetingly, before quickly walking out of the room and out of his house. 'Ten minutes,' she heard him call as she shut his door.

Sure enough, ten minutes later they sat down to breakfast. He was showered, shaved and dressed in a navy suit, with a chambray shirt and a bright, colourful tie.

'These muffins are incredible. I hadn't forgotten your cooking abilities but my tastebuds had. Thank you for reminding them.' He drank his coffee and reached for another muffin.

Janet swelled with happiness at his compliments. She forgave him for being late. She'd forgive him anything if he kept complimenting her like that.

He helped her to stack the dishwasher and clean up before they bundled into their coats and set off on the two-block walk to the clinic.

'You said that Mr Davies is coming to see me today. What other patients should I expect?'

'A lot of curious ones.' Janet laughed. 'I told Karen, our secretary, that it wouldn't be definite that you would be starting today. After all, you only arrived back in the country seventy-two hours ago.'

'I don't suffer from jet lag,' he informed her. 'Besides, you were probably ninety-nine per cent sure I'd take the job just as I had the same odds on you accepting me.'

'Good ol' Hamish,' Janet said, and they both laughed. 'Karen said she'd keep the patients to a minimum just in case you weren't able to start.'

'Make sure that any patients who book in throughout the course of the day see me. That way, *you* can be the one taking it easy for a change,' he ordered.

'Who's the boss here?' she asked, and smiled up at him as they walked up the driveway to the surgery. She unlocked the door and quickly entered the alarm code.

'It rings directly to the police station so it's imperative that we don't forget to switch it off. If it's tripped accidentally, the station's number is in the speed dial on all phones.'

'Who has keys and access?' he asked as he followed her through the renovated old house.

'Me and Karen, and Hamish has a spare set just in case. There's a set for you, as well as a mobile phone complete with preprogrammed numbers for police, hospital—'

'Hamish,' he added with a grin.

'But of course.' They smiled again.

'Good morning.' Karen walked in through the front door and introduced herself to Angus. She was a little bit shorter than Janet and had short red hair. 'Pleased to meet you, Angus. I can definitely see the strong family resemblance. Any more brothers hiding away somewhere?'

'Karen has been with the clinic since it opened two years ago,' Janet said by way of explanation.

'I'm cheerful, efficient and a brilliant crowd controller,' Karen added as she took her place behind the counter.

'I wouldn't have thought otherwise.' Angus nodded. 'And, sorry, there's just big brother Hamish and myself.'

'Their father is just as good-looking,' Janet added, and then blushed at what she'd said.

'So you think I'm good-looking?' Angus teased.

'You know you are,' she shrugged, hoping he wouldn't read anything into it.

Karen tilted her head to the side and said, 'It must have certainly given you all a common bond—the fact that both sets of parents are archaeologists and work together.'

'We all understand what it's like to have parents who are preoccupied with their work.'

'And when they're not so preoccupied, they interfere in your life because they've got nothing better to do.' Angus groaned in mock frustration. 'At least while my mother is working I don't have to listen to lectures on planting roots and settling down.'

'Aw,' Janet teased him back, hoping to cover the fact

that she thought his mother had a point. 'Does Angus's mummy pick on him?'

'Doesn't she get on Hamish's case as well?' Karen asked, and Angus shook his head.

'Hamish is settled and in a stable job. If you looked in a dictionary, besides the word ''settled'' it would have Hamish's name. Besides, we all assume he'll marry Leesa one day. She wouldn't let him marry anyone else.'

'That's true,' Janet added. 'I just wonder how much longer she has to wait.'

The bell above the door tinkled as it was opened, and the first patient for the day walked in.

'Good morning, Mrs Hay.' Janet smiled warmly at one of her favourite patients. Seventy-nine-year-old Mrs Hay had hypertension and came in once a week to have her blood pressure checked. 'This is our new doctor, Angus O'Donnell. He'll be with us for the next six months.'

The bell over the door tinkled again and another patient came in.

'Looks as though the day has begun,' Karen said, and gave both doctors their files.

'Come on, Dr O'Donnell,' Janet said over her shoulder. 'I'll give you a quick tour before we throw you into the lion's den.'

The morning progressed rapidly and by lunchtime the few appointments Karen kept available for daily callers were all filled. Janet saw Angus in the kitchen after she'd finished with yet another patient displaying mild flu symptoms.

'Flu, hay fever, flu, hay fever,' she said with a groan and sat down at the table opposite him.

''Tis the season,' he said. 'Let me get you a coffee.' He stood and walked to the bench where the urn was bubbling with water. He spooned instant coffee into a cup and added water. 'That's one thing I'd like to talk to you about.'

'What? Flu?'

'No. The coffee. Is it possible to have something *other* than this instant stuff?'

Janet smiled. 'If I get a coffee-machine, will you consider a permanent position here?'

Angus turned quickly to face her, his forehead creased into a frown. She saw him scan the smile on her face before he shrugged and turned back to stirring the coffee. 'That's not a very high price to pay for my services. One coffee-machine.'

'It's a start.' Janet accepted the cup he offered her and took a sip. 'So tell me how your morning was.'

'Not bad. A lot of questions from some patients, none from others. One lady, after discovering I was single, asked me when our wedding was going to be.'

Janet nearly sprayed the coffee across the room at his words. She gulped, coughed and smiled. 'That would be Mrs Thomas. She's been asking me for the past two years when I plan on settling down. Although she doesn't mind seeing a female doctor, she's of the conviction that a woman's place is in the home.'

'Mr Davies is due to see me next. Any last words of encouragement?'

'No.' Janet shook her head in disgust. 'If you told him he needed a sex change, he'd probably book himself in for the procedure on your say-so alone. Me? Try to get the man to take medication for his arthritis—or anything else for that matter—and he acts as though I'm trying to harm him. You're welcome to him.'

'Thanks.' Angus stood and placed his hands on Janet's shoulders. 'You're tense. You're supposed to relax now that I'm here, not stress out even more. Let's eat lunch so we can get the afternoon over and done with, then I'll take you out to dinner.'

The simple touch of his hands sent her pulses racing.

Janet tried not to flinch from the contact. It wasn't that Angus repulsed her—quite the opposite—it was just that she could quite easily get used to having him in her life on a more permanent basis. His hands worked their magic and she felt the tension in her neck begin to ease.

'Since when did you become a masseur?' she asked, her eyes closed.

His rich laugh caressed her. 'In China. I worked at a European clinic about four years ago. A masseuse shared the clinic rooms and she taught me the ancient art.'

'I just bet she did,' Janet mumbled under her breath. The warm and cosy feeling vanished into thin air at the mention of another woman. She sprang to her feet.

'Thanks,' she said bluntly, unable to meet his gaze. 'If we don't eat lunch soon, we won't get to eat at all.' She went to the refrigerator and pulled out some sandwiches she'd made that morning and carried to work in her bag.

'Here you are.' She handed him a plateful. 'Roast chicken with salad.'

'All right.' He took a bite. 'Yep. You're a brilliant cook, Dr Stevenson.'

After they'd finished lunch, they went to their separate consulting rooms and began the afternoon clinic. Soon after, there was a knock at Janet's door. Her patient had just left and she quickly finished writing up the notes. 'Come in,' she called, and felt her jaw nearly drop to the ground as Angus ushered Mr Davies in.

Janet stood, completely composed. 'What can I do for you, Dr O'Donnell?'

'I was wondering if I could get a second opinion from you as you're more experienced with this sort of query.'

Janet indicated the chairs and invited both men to sit down. What was Angus up to?

'Mr Davies has shown me a troublesome spot on his arm which he thinks might be skin cancer. As I've been working for the past few years in countries where skin cancer is not prevalent, I thought I'd ask your opinion. Mr Davies assured me it wasn't necessary to bother you but I explained the importance of a correct diagnosis, especially where *any* question of cancer is concerned.'

Janet's lips twitched but she managed to suppress the urge to smile. 'Mr Davies, would you mind rolling up your sleeve again?' She waited for him to comply.

'I told Dr O'Donnell it wasn't necessary for me to see you. You haven't done me much good in the past so I don't see why I need to see you now. You've finally taken my advice and employed a *real* doctor and the instant I see him he drags me back in here to see you again.'

'And as I've informed you on several occasions, Mr Davies,' Janet replied with a smile on her face and her voice as sweet as sugar, 'you're more than welcome to go to another surgery for a second opinion if you're not comfortable with my diagnoses. Now, Dr O'Donnell has thought it advisable for me to give *him* a second opinion regarding the mole on your arm.'

Mr Davies was still reluctant to show her his arm. When he'd been sick in the past with a respiratory tract infection, it had taken a great deal of persuasion for him to accept the antibiotics Janet had prescribed. She'd also managed to bully him into having his hands X-rayed to check the rate of arthritis in his fingers. It was getting to the stage where he would need the care of an orthopaedic surgeon as well as a rheumatologist.

At least with Angus here now, she would be assured of Mr Davies receiving the treatment he needed. It made her wonder just how long he'd been worried about this mole on his arm. If it *was* skin cancer, she hoped his prejudices against her gender wouldn't be the deciding factor in treatment coming too late to do any good.

'I'm sure,' Janet continued, 'that Dr O'Donnell has explained the importance of regular skin checks. The most serious type of skin cancer, Mr Davies, is what we term a melanoma. They appear as new moles or freckles. In the early stages they are flat and spread irregularly and are generally coloured black, red or bluish,' Janet said softly but firmly. She knew she had to be blunt with Mr Davies in order to get the urgency of her message across.

'They're very serious and can cause death by spreading to distant parts of the body such as the brain or lungs. Do you understand the importance of having this checked out?'

Mr Davies's complexion had turned a little pale at her last words.

'It can be very serious,' Angus added, 'which is why we need the second opinion from Dr Stevenson. She's had much more experience with this than I have.'

Both doctors waited in silence for the war that seemed to be going on inside Mr Davies to come to a conclusion. With obvious reluctance, he began to roll up his sleeve. Janet stood and walked over to him. She pulled her pocket torch out and switched it on.

'Thank you,' she said softly. She took a quick look, before saying, 'Angus. Pass me the magnifying glass from the second drawer, please.'

He did and she looked again. Angus looked as well.

'It does look like a melanoma,' she finally said. Mr Davies seemed ready to pass out at the news.

'W-what now?' he asked quietly, his previous bluster gone.

'We'd like you to have a biopsy. That's when a small sample of tissue is taken for microscopic examination. The removed tissue is soaked in molten paraffin wax and allowed to harden into a block. It is then cut into very thin slices and mounted on a glass slide for staining and examination,' Janet explained.

'This will tell us exactly what we're dealing with,' Angus added. 'If it's been caught in time, then removal of the mole is all that will be required.'

'I'll leave you in Dr O'Donnell's capable hands,' Janet said as she went to the door and held it open for the two men. 'He'll organise everything for you.'

As she shut the door behind them, Janet hoped that Mr Davies hadn't left it too late. If that mole had been there for quite some time, then the prognosis might not be all that good.

Her next patient was becoming a regular as well. Hannah Kellerman had given birth six months previously to a healthy baby boy. Her husband had left her just before the end of her third trimester and she had no family in the area to help her out.

'Come on in, Hannah,' Janet welcomed her. 'How's Sam today?'

'He has a temperature. I've given him paracetamol but it hasn't done any good. Would you mind taking a look at him?'

'Certainly.' Janet accepted the small babe from his mother and cradled him in her arms. 'What seems to be the problem, Master Kellerman? Aren't you feeling too good?' Janet sat down, holding him comfortably and firmly on her lap, before slowly unbuttoning his stretchsuit.

Placing the thermometer under his arm, she gave his little head a kiss as he started to protest. 'Shh. It's all right, little one. We'll sort you out.' She looked up at Hannah. 'How has he been feeding?'

'He's been a little bit fussy in the past two days.'

'No sign of any rash?'

'No.' Hannah shook her head for emphasis.

'How long has he had the temperature?'

'Just over three hours. I followed what my book says

about trying to bring the temperature down but nothing's worked. I was so relieved when Karen said you could see me straight away. She told me you had a new doctor starting today but I insisted on seeing you.' She fidgeted with Sam's favourite toy, before saying, 'You know us so well. I wouldn't feel comfortable with anyone else. They'd probably label me a neurotic mother.'

'You've done the right thing,' Janet confirmed. 'Better a neurotic mother than an uncaring one.' The thermometer beeped and Janet looked at the readout. 'Thirty-eight point seven. You poor darling.'

'What could it be, Dr Stevenson?' Hannah began to wring her hands together.

'Let's have a little look around,' Janet replied, and laid Sam on the examination couch. 'Has he had any diarrhoea or vomiting?'

'No.'

'What about solid food? Has he been eating that?'

'No. He's only wanted to drink from me but I'm down to giving him only a few feeds a day now.'

Janet reached for her pocket torch and tried to get Sam to open his mouth. He protested strongly at her prodding and did exactly what she wanted him to do. He opened his mouth and wailed in protest.

'His throat is quite red. I'd say he has an infection.' She placed a speculum over her otoscope and checked both of Sam's ears and his nose. 'Everything else looks healthy at this stage, although I'd guess his ears may be a little bit sore.'

Sam was really crying now and Janet quickly picked him up and cuddled him. 'It's all over, darling. It's all over,' she crooned, before handing him back to Hannah.

'I'll prescribe some antibiotics for him and that should clear things up.'

'How do I give Sam the antibiotics? Is it a pill?'

'No. It's a liquid. When you're at the chemist, purchase a medicine dropper. The millilitres will be marked on the side of the dropper and you give it to him the same way as liquid paracetamol.'

'Can he have paracetamol as well?'

'Yes. Keep giving it to him four-hourly until the temperature breaks.'

'How can I break the temperature?' Hannah asked with worry. 'I've done everything I can and it still hasn't worked.' She paced around the room, holding Sam close to her as he slowly stopped crying.

'Give him one dose of the antibiotics immediately and then another after ten o'clock tonight. Keep up with the paracetamol and keep bathing him. Don't worry about trying to get food into him—just keep his fluids up. If that means he feeds only from you, that's fine. As soon as you get home, dress him in a nappy and singlet only. Ensure the room is warm but not hot. Also, make sure that *you* drink plenty and try to eat something, even if it's just a piece of bread. If you don't keep your strength up, you'll be no good to Sam.'

Janet wrote the prescription out. 'Call through to the clinic as soon as his temperature breaks,' she instructed. After all, the girl had no one else to help her. 'If he's still hot in another few hours, call anyway and I'll come around and take another look at him.

'It looks as though he's gone to sleep now. That's also a good sign. It means his body can recharge its battery to fight off the germs that are causing the temperature.' Janet handed the script over. 'Everything clear?' she asked.

'Yes, Dr Stevenson. I'll call Karen if I have any further questions.'

'You let me know when it breaks,' Janet reiterated.

'I will, I promise.' She placed Sam tenderly into his
pram. 'Thank you so much, Dr Stevenson. I honestly don't
know how I would have coped during the past eight months
without your support.'

'That's why I'm here.' Janet nodded, a smile on her face.
Hannah wheeled the pram out and Janet began to write up
her notes. She'd tried on several occasions to get Hannah
into a support group for first-time mothers but Hannah had
declined.

'Everyone would ask questions. Why am I a single
mother? Where's Sam's father? Where's your family? No.
I just couldn't cope.'

The young mother had been so distraught that Janet
hadn't brought it up after the last outburst. As Hannah had
been coming to this practice since before she'd become
pregnant, she obviously felt comfortable talking to her GP
and Janet respected this.

After her next patient, there was another knock at the
door and Angus strolled in.

'Thanks for your help with Mr Davies.' His eyes twin-
kled with merriment.

Janet shook her head. 'Did you *really* need a second
opinion?'

'It's always better to be safe than sorry, especially where
melanomas are concerned,' he replied.

'What can I do for you?' she asked.

'I have no further patients this afternoon so I thought I'd
pick up the car Hamish has organised and see about hiring
some furniture—and, of course, pick up some coffee.'

'Among other things.'

'I'll be knocking on your front door at eight o'clock
sharp to take you out to dinner.'

'It's not necessary, Angus.'

'You're wrong, Janet. It's very necessary,' he responded, his eyes still twinkling with mischief, before leaving her to finish her work.

CHAPTER THREE

WHEN Janet arrived home, she made herself a cup of coffee and sat down to reflect on her day. Thankfully, Hannah Kellerman had called through an hour after leaving the surgery to say that Sam's temperature had broken and he was more settled than before. Janet had breathed a sigh of relief, glad that Sam's little body was coping with the infection.

The phone rang and she picked up the receiver. 'Dr Stevenson.'

'Why didn't you call me?' Leesa asked, a smile in her voice.

'Sorry,' Janet mumbled. 'I guess I forgot.'

'Must have been a good night, then,' Leesa fished.

'Yes. I've forgotten how much fun Angus can be.'

'Fun, eh?'

'Get your mind out of the gutter,' Janet said in her best big-sister voice. 'We're friends.'

'Oh you're back to denial again. It doesn't work, Janet. Admit once and for all that you're attracted to him and you'll be doing yourself a big favour. It's OK, you know.' Leesa's voice was calm and soothing. 'It's OK to have these feelings for Angus. If he kissed you then I'm sure he has similar feelings.'

'It's all a bit too cosy. Working together, living next door to each other.' Janet thought for a moment, before saying, 'You knew, didn't you? You knew Hamish had told him he could stay here.'

'Yes, but I didn't expect this sudden attraction to spark between the two of you.'

'It's too late now. He's here. Taking over my life,' Janet said with resignation.

'Where is he now?' Leesa asked.

'Out leasing furniture and buying things.'

'You sound a little down.' Leesa had picked up Janet's mood. 'Hey, I've got a great idea. I actually have the night off so how about I come over and you can cook us a great meal? We'll get some videos or go out to the movies and just have some sister time.'

'Ah… Gee, Leesa. That's a…great offer…' Janet fumbled, not at all sure how to tell her sister the truth. 'But as it turns out…I…um, well, I already have plans for this evening.'

'Angus?' Leesa guessed.

'Well, yes. He's taking me out to dinner.'

'That's all right. I should be studying anyway.'

'Sorry, Leesa.'

'Don't apologise. I'll tell Hamish I need help and at least that way I can get him over here for dinner.'

'*You're* going to cook?' Janet couldn't resist teasing.

'No. Hamish orders Chinese or Thai and brings it with him. He's still recovering from the one time I did cook him a meal and that was at least five years ago.'

They both laughed. Janet possessed the ability to throw some ingredients together and it always turned out tasting incredible. Leesa couldn't boil water without burning it. On the other hand, Leesa was a brilliant seamstress and could turn any piece of material into the latest designer fashions. Janet found it difficult to sew on a button.

'Listen, Leesa. I'd better go and get ready. I have a few things to get done before he picks me up.'

'Sure, but remember—don't fight it, Janet. The O'Donnell brothers are impossible to resist.' They rang off.

Janet sat there for a moment, thinking about Leesa's words. Karen, too, had seen through her 'we're just friends' statement. Standing up, Janet went into the bathroom and started the shower.

Karen had teased her about her 'date' with Angus, and Janet had brushed the suggestion away with her hand.

'We're old friends.'

'You had dinner together last night. Breakfast together this morning and now—'

'How did you know about…?' Janet had trailed off as Karen's smile had grown wider.

'Angus raved about your muffins. Asked me if I'd tried any before. So when is it my turn to have breakfast with the boss?'

'The man had no food in his house. What was I supposed to do? Let him starve?'

'Heaven forbid,' Karen joked as she placed a hand over her heart. 'So where do you think he'll take you tonight?'

'I have no idea.' Janet looked at her appointment book for the following day, pretending not to be interested in the conversation.

'How will you decide what to wear? I always hate it when guys don't tell you what type of clothing you should choose.'

Janet looked blankly at Karen. 'You know, I haven't even thought about it.'

Karen consulted the clock. 'It's six o'clock. Too late to go and buy a new outfit.'

'Oh, stop it,' Janet demanded on a giggle. 'I'm not going to buy a new dress just for Angus. How many times do I have to tell you that we're just friends? We've known each other for an eternity. We're like brother and sister.'

'Then you wouldn't mind if I asked him out on a date?' Karen asked, her face serious.

Janet opened her mouth to inform Karen that she would have no trouble with that but the words stuck in her throat and a nauseating feeling swamped her. She sat down.

'I guess you would mind,' Karen added with a smile. 'You can tell me until you're blue in the face that you and

Angus are just friends, but stop lying to yourself. That may have been the case in the past but not any more. The air simply crackles when the two of you are in the same room.'

'Am I that obvious? No,' she added a moment later. 'Don't answer that.'

'Everything will work itself out,' Karen responded cheerfully. 'The more pertinent question is, what are you going to wear tonight that will knock Angus O'Donnell fair and square in the solar plexus?'

They discussed Janet's wardrobe in detail and finally decided on a mid-thigh-length black dress with short sleeves. It was elegant and classical. Although it was the middle of winter and went against all her sensibilities, Janet agreed. Stockings and high heels were essential, as was the shawl she draped over her arms.

They'd be in heated areas for most of the night, so she wasn't too bothered about the blustering winds outside.

'Vanity, vanity. All is vanity,' she told her reflection when she twirled in front of the mirror, giving herself one final check. She'd arranged her hair on top of her head with a few loose tendrils coming down, and looped gold hoops through her pierced ear lobes.

When the doorbell rang a few minutes later, Janet felt butterflies flutter around in the pit of her stomach. 'It's only Angus,' she told herself firmly.

Hurrying to the door, she opened it and, without looking at him, quickly ushered him inside.

'It's rather cold out tonight,' he remarked as they stood in the hallway. Simultaneously, their gazes met and held. Both seemed dazed at the transformation of the other. Beneath his thick scarf and winter coat, which hung open, Angus looked impeccable in a black dinner suit and white shirt. His bow-tie was the exact colour of his eyes—a deep, mesmerising blue.

'You look...' His voice trailed off. It was soft and gentle, and settled over Janet like a caress. His eyes seemed to devour her like a man starved of food. 'Stunning,' he finished. Belatedly, he held out a bunch of flowers. 'These are for you.'

'Freesias.' Janet was amazed. The mix of colours was vibrant. 'How did you know?'

'That these are your favourite?' he asked with a smug and satisfied smile. When she nodded he shrugged, trying to appear nonchalant. 'I remembered.'

'From when?' Janet cradled the bouquet in her arms, her romantic sensibility working in overdrive at his sweet and thoughtful gesture. Tears pricked at her eyes and she quickly turned away and headed for the kitchen. She draped her shawl over a chair as she walked past the table, getting it out of the way.

'From the time we were all stuck at your parents' house one evening when that terrible storm broke.'

'I remember the occasion and the storm but not how you learned my favourite flower.' Janet couldn't look at him. If she did, she *would* break down into tears of happiness so instead she searched around for a vase and filled it with water.

'We'd all managed to make it over for dinner. Mum and Dad, Hamish and myself. You were in your first year of medical school and Leesa's crush on Hamish was starting to turn serious. After dinner, as our parents started talking shop, the four of us went and had a game of pool. Leesa started the questions while we were playing and had us all name our favourite food, drink, colour and flower, among other things.'

Janet carefully arranged the flowers and looked up at Angus. 'She was trying to get information embedded into Hamish's subconscious—not yours.' Janet smiled and looked at her beautiful freesias again. 'That was quite a long time ago, Angus. You *are* full of surprises.'

He cleared his throat. 'To tell the truth, Janet, your choice of flower stuck in my memory. I thought it admirable that it wasn't roses or carnations as so many other women preferred. Freesias were different. In fact, I even recall commending you on your choice at the time.'

Janet laughed. 'Isn't it strange how there are some things the mind just never forgets?'

Angus looked down at his watch. 'We'd better be going. We have reservations for eight-thirty.'

Janet collected her bag and shawl, allowing Angus to usher her through the house, turning off lights as he went. At the door, he helped her into her thick coat and warm scarf.

'Your chariot, *mademoiselle*,' he announced as they walked down her garden path and out to the road. Janet had expected him to suggest taking her car but there on the road stood his leased car. A midnight-blue Jaguar.

'Wow!' She couldn't contain her surprise. 'When you lease a car, Angus, you really *lease a car!* What kind is it?' He held the door for her and Janet slipped inside. The leather upholstery was smooth and very comfortable. She did her seat belt up and waited for him to take his place beside her in the driver's seat.

'It's an S-Type.' His smile was wide with boyish excitement. 'The latest model. Hamish had organised a Jaguar Sovereign, like his own car, but this is more *me*.'

He drove carefully through the busy streets and into the heart of Newcastle. They stopped and parked the car next to the grandest restaurant—Elizabeth's.

It was situated on the foreshore and had a reputation for the best seafood in town.

'If you're trying to impress me, Angus…it's working,' Janet said softly as they walked through the door.

'Good evening, sir, madam,' the *maître d'* greeted them. 'Your coats, please?' After taking their coats and confirming their reservations, he led them to a quiet table near the open fireplace.

'I am,' Angus stated once they'd been left alone. 'I am trying to impress you, but most of all I'm trying to say thank you. For the accommodation, the job—your company.' He reached for her hand and kissed it gently. 'Coming home for a spell was just what I needed.'

For a spell. His words stung her and the romantic atmosphere disintegrated into thin air. Janet slowly withdrew her hand and accepted the menu the waiter handed her.

She stared unseeingly at the words before her. Karen had definitely been right. There was much more between her and Angus than she'd been willing to admit. Oh, sure, she'd felt the attraction between them but it went even beyond that.

If she allowed herself to be carried away on the joyride Angus was sweeping her up in, she'd only be setting herself up for heartbreak when he left in six months' time.

During the past twenty-four hours, since his return into her life, Janet had held in the back of her mind the possibility that she might be able to convince him to stay. Now, considering a few of his comments, she doubted whether even *she* had the power to exert over him the need to settle down. Plant roots.

'What will you have?' he asked.

Janet raised her eyes to his, clearing her thoughts and bringing herself back to the present.

'Ah.' She glanced back down at the menu and pasted a smile on her face. 'I'm not sure. What would you suggest?'

'Lobster sounds wonderful.'

'Great.'

'How about some prawns for starters?'

'Sure.' Janet was now past caring what was ordered and doubted whether she'd appreciate the taste of anything right at this moment, but when the food arrived she found it irresistibly mouth-watering and scrumptious.

She allowed herself to relax—slightly—enjoying Angus's sharp wit and listening to more stories of his time overseas. From what he was saying, he'd worked everywhere. But only for six months at a time.

It was as though he were laying the foundation for her. His casual caresses on her hands and the way his eyes seemed to devour her with desire were signals that he wouldn't mind changing their relationship. Yet at the same time he was ensuring that she knew it would only be an affair. An affair for six months.

They finished their meal, and after Angus had taken care of the bill, they walked back to his car bundled once again in their thick winter coats.

'At least it's not raining,' he remarked as he settled her into the passenger seat.

They were both quiet on the drive home, content to listen to the soft classical music to which Angus had tuned the radio. He garaged the car and came around to open her door.

'Thank you.' She accepted his hand and he walked her to her front door. 'You've spoilt me thoroughly tonight, Angus. It was lovely.'

He waited until she'd unlocked the door before replying. 'Glad you enjoyed it.' He bent his head for a kiss. It was soft and gentle. He made no effort to deepen it and for a split second Janet wondered whether she'd read his earlier signals incorrectly. 'Sleep well. I'll see you at the clinic in the morning.'

With that, he turned and walked to his own front door. Janet went inside, even more confused than before.

Perhaps all Angus was offering was friendship? Perhaps she was allowing her own feelings to whirl out of control? Perhaps she should stop listening to Karen's nonsense!

She went into her bedroom and undressed, before brushing her hair and getting ready for bed. As she lay down she heard Angus's shower start. Thoughts of him naked, standing beneath the warmth of the spray, began to converge on her mind.

It was the last thing she wanted or needed when she was in this frame of mind. She could imagine all too clearly how it would feel to share a shower with him. To have him deepen that kiss and take her on a whirlwind of sensual exploration.

She buried her head beneath the pillow, forcing her thoughts into order. Finally the water stopped and after a few more minutes there was silence from the house next door.

'Let me know if the rash persists, Mr Windsor, and I'll prescribe a different cream.'

'Right you are, Doctor,' Mr Windsor said, before he stood up and walked out of her consulting room. Janet wrote up the notes and checked her patient list to see who was next.

She'd managed to keep her distance from Angus during the past two weeks he'd been back in her life. Her feelings had been swinging out of control ever since their initial dinner to discuss the locum position. Janet needed time to come to terms with her changing emotions. From seeing him as a brother to a…lover? She wasn't sure what role she wanted to play in his life or what role, if any, he would play in hers. What she did know was that whenever he walked into a room her entire body came to life with such a burning desire it scared her.

On a cold Friday morning she arrived at the clinic at the crack of dawn as she'd been unable to sleep because of dreams of Angus and herself in a spa bath. The dreams were becoming more regular and more potent. She felt like blushing every time she looked at him.

When he arrived she was buried in paperwork. He stuck his head around her door and waited for her to look at him. She mentioned that she was swamped and had to get things organised before the patients arrived, effectively brushing him off.

When he'd closed the door, she felt guilty for a moment but also realised that her words were true. If she didn't concentrate, the administrative work would never get done. Karen was a marvel and ran the practice with well-ordered precision but there were some things that required Janet's attention. Drug ordering and which companies to order from. Which hospital offered the best treatment for her patients. Signing the letters she'd dictated. Budgets. The list went on and on. Not that she minded. After all, this was *her* practice and this way she could run it the way *she* wanted to.

Late that afternoon, as she was prescribing yet another antibiotic for secondary infections allied to flu symptoms, Janet heard Karen calling loudly.

'Janet! Angus!' Her voice was firm, loud and urgent.

Janet threw down her pen and rushed to the door, her patient following her.

Karen was in the waiting room, kneeling on the floor beside Mr Campbell.

'I think it's a heart attack,' she told Janet as Angus came rushing in to the room.

'Phone for an ambulance,' she instructed Karen as she loosened Mr Campbell's tie and undid his shirt buttons. Angus loosened the man's trousers. 'Breathing's stopped. Pulse is weak. Patient has a history of angina pectoris,' she told Angus.

As she had her fingers pressed to his carotid pulse, she felt it fade out. 'Pulse is gone.'

Immediately she turned his head to the side to clear his airway, before tipping his head right back, pinching the nose and beginning mouth-to-mouth resuscitation. Angus counted her breaths and intervened with cardiac massage.

'Ambulance is on its way,' Karen informed them, and started ushering the few waiting patients into the kitchen. 'Come and have a cup of tea,' she said soothingly. Janet was thankful for Karen's action and made a mental note to tell her so.

After a few minutes Janet checked again for a pulse. She was beginning to tire, and knew that if a pulse wasn't present then she and Angus would need to swap places. Mr Campbell gave a weak cough as his chest began to rise and fall by itself. 'Pulse is faint, but there,' she reported.

His eyelids fluttered open briefly and she smiled down at him. 'Everything is fine now. Dr O'Donnell and I are still here. We won't leave you. Everything is going to be all right. Close your eyes and rest now.' Her patient did as he was told.

'No allergies to morphine or prochlorperazine?' Angus asked.

'His chart is on Karen's desk.' Janet continued her observations of Mr Campbell as Angus checked the notes, before going to the drug storage room. Within a few minutes he returned and knelt down again.

'The pulse is strengthening. Let's turn him into the coma position.' After ensuring he was comfortable, she watched Angus draw up the shot.

'Mr Campbell,' she said clearly, 'Dr O'Donnell is going to give you an injection now. It will help you relax and relieve the pain. It will also help reduce the nausea you're no doubt feeling. Just stay still. Everything is going to be fine.'

She placed an oxygen mask over his face and told him

to breathe slowly. After a few more minutes he was in a relaxing sleep. The morphine was obviously taking effect.

It was another ten minutes before the ambulance arrived. The paramedics transferred Mr Campbell to the stretcher and wheeled him to the ambulance.

'I'll go with him. Ask Karen to contact his daughter—it's in his file.' She raised her eyes to meet his. 'Looks as though your holiday is over now.' She smiled. He returned her smile and Janet felt her knees weaken.

'Your patients are in good hands.'

'I know. Thanks for your help. It makes life a lot easier, having another doctor around.'

'How on earth did you survive without me?' he teased.

Janet climbed into the ambulance beside Mr Campbell and gave Angus a small wave as the paramedics closed the double doors. Soon they were travelling through the streets, sirens wailing, heading for Newcastle General.

The paramedics had hooked Mr Campbell up to the electrocardiograph and Janet sat there, monitoring the readouts. She held her patient's hand and spoke comfortingly to him, yet in the back of her mind Angus's words were causing her stress.

How *had* she survived without him? As a doctor, she knew she'd coped until things had become too difficult which was why she was looking for a partner. She supposed she should take Angus at his word that he would only be staying six months and continue to look for a permanent partner for the practice, although there was still the hope deep within her heart that Angus would stay.

How had *she* survived without him? Until he'd waltzed back into her life, she hadn't known her life had been missing anything. Now…now she knew she was missing something, but was Angus the answer? Was he her soul mate?

Janet knew she was classified as a hopeless romantic. She believed there was someone perfect for everyone out there and she knew she'd never settle for second best. Leesa was the same, except that Leesa had found her soul mate. All her baby sister had to do now was to convince Hamish that they were meant to be together.

Was it the same for her and Angus? She knew he felt the magnetic pull that existed between them. It was overwhelmingly powerful but was it too powerful for her to fight? After all, Angus might be attracted to her but that didn't mean he would willingly sacrifice his carefree existence for her. Would he?

As the ambulance slowed, Janet forced her thoughts back to the present. Mr Campbell was still sleeping soundly. She knew that he stood a good chance of recovery but only if he was able to make it through the next hour in similar form. If another infarction were to occur, his chances would diminish rapidly.

He was wheeled out and taken directly to ICU. Janet spoke with the doctor and sister in charge, passing on details and signing notes. Karen had phoned a message through to the ICU to say that Mr Campbell's daughter was on her way. Thankfully, she hadn't tried to use Janet's mobile phone. Although she had it with her, there were certain areas in the hospital where mobile phones were not permitted to be switched on as they could interfere with the very sensitive equipment that helped keep patients alive.

Janet waited for Natalie Campbell-Hirst to arrive, knowing a familiar face would help in these distressing circumstances. Fifteen minutes later, Janet saw her walk slowly into ICU.

'Natalie.' Janet crossed to her side. Natalie Campbell-Hirst was a tall woman in her early forties. She was happily married with two teenage sons and worked as a legal secretary for her husband. She was always a happy person but at the moment she looked like a scared little girl.

'Oh, Dr Stevenson. Thank goodness you're here. Is he all right?'

'He's stabilised. I'm sure Karen told you that he had a heart attack in the waiting room. Dr O'Donnell, my new locum, and I were on hand immediately. Your father has received prompt attention and, depending on how he progresses within the next half-hour, should make a complete recovery.'

'Thank you.' Natalie clutched at Janet's hand. 'Can I see him?'

'Of course, but only for a few minutes. He's been sleeping comfortably for a while now, which is a very good sign. It means his body is relaxed and therefore in a good state to recover. Remember,' Janet whispered as she led Natalie over to her father's bed, 'no excitement.'

At Janet's nod of encouragement, Natalie called softly to her father. It took a few seconds before his eyes fluttered open.

'Natalie?' His voice was barely audible but they both heard him.

'I'm here, Dad.' Tears formed in her eyes and she clutched at his hand, giving it a little squeeze. 'Dr Stevenson's here and says that everything is going to be just fine.'

Mr Campbell gave a small nod, before closing his eyes again and drifting back into a healing sleep.

'Why don't you sit down for a few minutes?'

Janet left them alone and returned to the nurses' desk. Picking up the internal phone, she dialled Leesa's beeper, then replaced the receiver.

A few seconds later the phone rang. 'Hi, Leesa.'

'What are you doing in ICU?' her sister asked.

'Admitting a patient. Got ten minutes spare for a cup of coffee?'

'Sure. I've just finished one theatre case but the next

one's not due to start for another half-hour. I'll meet you in the cafeteria in five.'

Janet replaced the receiver and thanked the nursing staff. She walked back to Mr Campbell's bedside and spoke in whispered tones to Natalie.

'I have to go now. I'll be in close contact with the hospital regarding your father's condition. If you have any questions or would just like to chat, give me a call. You have my numbers, don't you?'

'Yes. Thanks again, Dr Stevenson. I…' She wiped another tear from her eyes. 'I'm just glad he's going to be all right.'

'He'll be fine. What he probably *won't* like is the change in lifestyle this heart attack will mean. More exercise. Giving up those doughnuts he loves so much. He's been lucky this time.'

'We'll do everything we can to help him.'

'Good. He's going to need the support of his family.'

'Thanks again.' Natalie held out her hand to shake Janet's.

Janet left ICU and went to the cafeteria. Leesa was dressed in theatre scrubs, sitting down at a table by herself with two cups of coffee in front of her. Janet sat down opposite her.

'Thanks, sis.' She accepted the cup. 'I need this.'

'So what's been happening?'

Janet quickly explained about Mr Campbell's admission and Leesa nodded.

'How's Angus settling in? Think you can get him to stay permanently?'

'Not a hope in the world.' Janet took another sip of her coffee. 'He's been back in my life for two weeks and three days and it feels as though he never left. Which is absurd,' Janet continued, not giving Leesa a chance to respond. 'He's been gone for over eight years and I've changed so much but still…' She trailed off and looked into her now empty cup.

'I don't believe it,' Leesa said with a silly smile on her face.

'What?' Janet asked, as though coming back to reality. Her feelings for Angus had her in such a tizz that she had a hard time controlling them.

'I've accepted that it happened to me, but *you?* Two Stevenson women is more than I can bear.'

'What are you talking about?'

'Angus. You've actually fallen in love with him.' Her sister shrugged matter-of-factly.

'I have not. I've admitted that I'm attracted to him but, no, I'm not in love with him,' Janet denied emphatically.

'Yes, you are. I can only recognise the symptoms because I'm in love with an O'Donnell as well.'

'You're talking nonsense.'

'Am I? Think of everything that's happened in the past few weeks since Angus came back into your life and then tell me there's nothing different.'

Janet thought for a long time, before turning amazed eyes to her sister. 'I don't believe it.'

'The sooner you come to terms with it, the sooner you can get on with your life.'

'Is that what you've done?' she asked Leesa. 'You seem to be living in limbo.'

'Hamish is more complicated than Angus. Besides, at the moment I have two more years before I qualify. Until then, Hamish will continue to regard me as the student he's mentored for the past ten years. Timing is very important with Hamish. He requires an intellectual equal as his wife and until I prove that, things continue the way they are.'

'I hope you're right.'

'Of course I am. I'm an authority on Hamish O'Donnell. The question is, what are we going to do about you?'

'There's nothing to do. Angus and I are friends who are attracted to each other.'

'Nothing more?'

'What more can there be? He's leaving in six months,' Janet said. 'He'll be gone and there's nothing I can do to make him stay. I'd just be setting myself up for heartbreak.'

Leesa had a smug smile on her face. 'So you *have* thought about it. Perhaps you haven't identified exactly what the feelings are that you have for Angus but, from what you've just said, can't *you* see that you're in love with him?'

Janet was silent for a moment, before facing the truth. Leesa was right. She wasn't just attracted to Angus—she was one hundred per cent in love with him already.

'Oh, Leesa. What am I going to do?' she wailed, and buried her head in her hands.

CHAPTER FOUR

THE revelation left Janet feeling far from elated as she let herself into her house later that evening. How could she have fallen in love with Angus so quickly? At the moment she felt highly irresponsible at finding herself in such a situation.

She went into the bathroom and stripped off, her body relaxing under the warm and inviting spray of the shower. Janet refused to think of Angus but, as hard as she tried to school her thoughts, it was to no avail.

Every time she closed her eyes she could clearly picture that taunting smile, turning her insides to mush. Those blue eyes... Her body shuddered involuntarily as she recalled how expressive his eyes had been as they'd sat across the table from each other at the restaurant the other week.

The message they'd conveyed had been, Stay with me—where you belong. There was no doubt in her mind that Angus wanted her. She also knew he simply wanted an affair.

She sighed and switched the taps off. Towelling herself dry, Janet dressed in a fleecy, pale pink tracksuit which had small flowers embroidered around the neckline and down the sides of the legs. Leesa had made it for her birthday last year which made Janet love it even more.

Just as she sat down in front of the pot-belly stove in the lounge room to towel her hair dry, there was a knock at her door.

'It's just me,' Angus called out as she made her way to the door. When she opened it, a blast of cold air gusted in and she quickly ushered Angus inside.

'I heard the shower going so I knew you were home,' he volunteered. 'Have you eaten?'

'No,' Janet replied as she turned and walked back into the lounge room.

'How about we order Chinese while I give you an update on this afternoon's clinic? In turn, you can tell me what happened at the hospital.'

Janet wasn't sure what to say—or what to do! How did a person behave when the love of their life walked unexpectedly into the room? She sat down, keeping her back to him.

'I'm not very hungry,' she replied, but at that instant, her stomach rumbled.

Angus laughed. 'Your stomach begs to differ. I'll order the Chinese. You just sit there and relax.' Angus walked out of the room and she heard him using her phone.

He just made himself right at home, she mused, and why shouldn't he, given their family history? It wasn't *his* fault that she'd fallen in love with him. How on earth did Leesa do it? Day in, day out in the company of the man she'd been in love with for years, and she still managed to string coherent sentences together, as well as keep up her hectic work schedule.

Janet shook her head and ran her fingers through her wet hair. She reached for the towel she'd left on the lounge and gave her scalp a vigorous rub.

'Won't you knot your hair, doing it like that?' Angus asked as he walked in and sat down beside her. Janet's back was still to him as he reached out and stilled her hands with his own. 'Here. Let me have a go.'

He picked up the comb she'd left on the coffee-table and slowly combed the knot in her hair out. Next, he gently began to dry her hair with the towel. Janet closed her eyes, her body burning with desire and heat from his touch. She kept her back rigid, although she could feel the pressure of his thigh at the base of her spine as he edged a little closer.

'So, I presume Mr Campbell is in a satisfactory condition?'

'Um…' Janet stopped and cleared her throat. 'Yes. Yes, he was doing fine when I left.'

'Did his daughter arrive quickly?'

'Uh-huh.' Janet gave a small nod. 'She was there not long after we arrived.'

'Good. Family comes first, especially in situations like this,' he replied.

'Oh, you're one to talk, Angus O'Donnell,' she teased.

'What's that supposed to mean?' he queried with a slight edge to his tone.

'How about the fact that every visit to your parents becomes shorter and shorter?'

'You know what my mother's like,' he said, his voice filled with annoyance. 'She constantly nags me about settling down.' The pressure on her hair increased a little and she reached up to stop his hands. Turning around to face him, Janet looked into his eyes. There was no denying it. She was definitely in love with him.

'Yes, Angus. I know what Mary's like. I also know that she only wants what's best for you. She's your mother. It's what every mother wants for their children.'

'She doesn't bother Hamish—just me. She doesn't even know *what* I do, yet she still criticises me.'

'Angus, you're a GP!'

He looked at her and shook his head. 'I keep forgetting you don't know,' he said quietly.

Janet frowned. 'Don't know what?' Something wasn't right here.

'Drop it.' He placed his hands on her shoulders and turned her back around, before resuming his ministrations on her hair.

'Fine. I don't know what's going on, but just for the record your mother does bother Hamish, Angus, but in a different way. We all know that Leesa is the perfect person for Hamish but he's the only one who can't see it. For years now your mother has been spouting Leesa's accomplishments in front of Hamish, hoping that he'd pick up on her words and see Leesa for the woman she's become. But as Leesa herself tells me, the timing is just not right yet.'

'She's very patient, your sister,' Angus observed, his composure back in place. 'I'm too impulsive. When I see something I want, I go for it. Life is too precious to waste, which is why I've spent my time seeing the world—doing the things *I* want to do and working for whomever I choose. Living my life to the fullest.'

Janet smiled. 'You don't need to travel the globe to live your life to the fullest, Angus. It's being true to your heart that counts. *That's* what your mother keeps pressuring you to do.'

'No, she doesn't.'

'If you were truly happy, Angus, her words wouldn't bother you.'

'Let's talk about something else.' His words were final.

'Sure. What did you have in mind?' Janet would've loved to have questioned him further but, considering his reluctance, she decided to follow his change of topic. After all, she didn't want to fight with him.

'Mr Davies's biopsy.'

'Wow, Angus. You really are a sweet talker.' Janet laughed.

'You ain't heard nothin' yet,' he returned, and she could tell he was smiling. 'The next round of tests begins on Monday. Because the initial biopsy was malignant, he'll have to undergo quite a bit more poking and prodding, as well as putting up with all sorts of females bothering him on a ''professional'' basis.' His tone sobered. 'It's sad that Mr Davies allowed his discrimination against females to stand in the way for too long.'

'He doesn't mean to make trouble—he's just not accustomed to how the world has changed. The fact is that some people feel more comfortable with a female doctor and some with a male, which is why most practices have at least one of each on the staff. It's necessary.'

'Thankfully for you, my dear Janet, I happened along at the right time to fill the void in your charming practice.'

'So what are your perceptions of the last couple of weeks, or shouldn't I ask?'

'Hmm, now, let me see,' Angus said in a thoughtful tone, before he continued, 'I think you've done an excellent job of setting the practice up. It runs smoothly and efficiently. Karen is a great receptionist and secretary and displayed those talents throughout today's emergency. I even like the renovated building. You were correct when you said it made the patients feel more like people than numbers. I worked in a ''number'' practice like that in New Zealand. Sure, they all made a lot of money, but it wasn't for me.'

'Some patients prefer that type of practice. They don't want to get to know the doctors on a personal level. There's something for everyone.' Janet felt a glow of happiness at his praise. His opinion mattered far too much and if he'd picked faults, as he'd done previously, she'd have probably burst into tears.

Janet relaxed a little and felt her back come into contact with his chest. He continued to gently rub her hair with the towel and then comb it through. They remained silent for quite a while, the touch of his skin against her causing tingles to spiral throughout her body in a frenzied state of excitement.

Opening her mouth, Janet tried to focus on some deep breathing exercises, hoping to calm the burning fire that was developing deep within her. The touch of his hand on her hair had now turned into a sexual caress and she closed her eyes with longing. She started to feel giddy, her body relaxing more against the firmness of his chest.

'Mmm,' she groaned softly when he rested his hands on her shoulders and gently began to massage them. Her tongue darted out to wet her dry lips, the deep-breathing exercises doing absolutely nothing to calm the desire that continued to grow.

As though in slow motion, Angus brushed her hair away from her neck, allowing his mouth access to her creamy-smooth skin.

Janet gasped when his lips finally made contact and she tipped her head to the side, revealing more neck for him to caress. She lifted her hand and threaded her fingers through his hair as he continued the onslaught.

Unable to believe the lack of control she had over her emotions, Janet decided the best course of action would be to ride the storm and see where it took her. Angus nibbled his way up to her ear lobe, being careful of the diamond and gold studs she wore.

Janet smiled, then shivered as goose-bumps tingled their way down her arm. She opened her eyes and turned her head a little more so their eyes could meet. She knew hers were filled with the same desire she saw in his.

'This is crazy,' she whispered.

'Crazy never felt so right before,' he replied, before claiming her lips in an electrifying kiss. Angus brought one hand up to cup her face as Janet swivelled in his embrace, their bodies now facing each other.

The building warmth of desire which had ignited in her body now came to life as the kiss turned from one of passion to one of hunger. She couldn't get enough of him—or him of her.

Janet tugged his shirt from his jeans, before running her

hands up the firmness of his warm chest. He groaned with delight and she gently ran her nails back down, before bringing her hands around to his back. He rewarded her with another consuming kiss.

Angus wrapped his arms about her, urging their bodies even closer. The smell of his aftershave only added to the mind-numbing sensuality and power he had over her. Janet nipped at his lips with her teeth, unable to believe what was happening.

The telephone rang in the same instant that the doorbell chimed.

Angus broke from the kiss and threw his head back, his eyes closed. Janet rested her head against his chest as the phone continued to ring and the doorbell chimed once more.

'You get the phone, I'll get the door,' he instructed as he slowly let her go and stood up.

Janet walked to the ringing phone, surprised that her legs supported her weight. They felt like jelly and the rest of her body was still burning with uncontrollable cravings for more of Angus O'Donnell.

'Hello,' she said almost sleepily into the receiver.

'Janet? Are you all right?' Leesa's voice came clearly down the line.

'Yeah, sis. I'm fine. Just a little tired after today's excitement.'

Leesa chuckled. 'With your patient or discovering you were in love with Angus?'

'Shh,' Janet said immediately. It was ridiculous. She knew Angus couldn't hear Leesa's end of the conversation but the words made her feel self-conscious. Angus was closing the door with his foot, his hands holding the bags containing their dinner. How much had he ordered?

Janet watched as he took it into the lounge room and

reappeared a few moments later, heading towards where she stood in the kitchen.

'Who is it?' he said quietly.

'Leesa,' Janet mouthed, watching as Angus rummaged in her drawers and cupboards for plates and utensils.

'So, to what do I owe the honour of this call?' Janet asked her sister, her eyes never leaving Angus. The way his jeans tightened over his behind when he bent to pick up a serviette he'd dropped. The way his untucked shirt hung casually around his waist. The way his eyes were still smouldering with desire when he looked at her.

'So is that all right with you?' Leesa finished.

'Is what all right with me?' Janet asked, and realised she wasn't paying her sister any attention at all. Angus realised what had happened and flashed Janet his winning smile, knowing he was distracting her. He walked back to the lounge room.

'Are you sure everything's all right?' Leesa asked again. 'You're acting very strange.'

'I'm fine.' Janet took a deep breath. 'It's just that Angus is here and, well…'

'Oh, I see.' Leesa giggled and Janet blushed.

'Angus has ordered Chinese as neither of us has eaten. That's all.' She whispered the last two words as Angus returned to the kitchen to collect two wineglasses. She watched yet again as he returned to the lounge room before he called out that he was just going next door for a moment.

Janet waited until the front door closed behind him.

'OK. Is what all right with me?'

'If Hamish and I came over for dinner tomorrow night. That way you get to show off your brilliant cooking skills to Angus and I get to spend some quality time with Hamish.'

'I…I don't know, Leesa,' Janet protested.

'Come on, Janet. The four of us haven't been together

since his return. He's the only surrogate brother I have, although if you have your way he could be my brother-in-law which is even better.'

'Oh, stop,' Janet ordered. 'Sure. Come for dinner. Seven-thirty and bring the drinks. I'll have everything else organised.'

'Knew I could count on you. Now, off you go and have a nice relaxing evening with Angus and you can tell me all the juicy details later.'

Angus walked back in through the front door as Janet replaced the receiver. He carried a bottle of red wine and motioned for her to join him.

When she returned to the lounge room she said, 'Leesa says...' She stopped and looked at the arrangement on the coffee-table. 'Hello,' she finished.

Angus had placed a cushion on either side of the table and had set it, complete with a few of her freesias in a small vase as a centrepiece. The food was set out, ready for them to help themselves, and Angus was pouring the wine.

'Sit.'

She did as she was told and waited for him to do the same.

His thoughtfulness at arranging everything, especially when he knew she liked this sort of thing—fresh flowers included—touched her deeply.

'The table looks great. You've thought of everything,' she pointed out.

'Yes, I have.' He raised his glass for a toast and she followed suit. 'To old friends. To new friends. To...' he lifted one eyebrow, a gleam in his eyes '...close friends.'

Janet clinked glasses with him but didn't respond. At that moment she felt as though she were in no man's land—in love with Angus, desperately wanting to be with him yet not wanting the affair she was positive was on his mind.

She sipped from her glass before he said, 'Eat up. It all has to go.'

'You've ordered way too much,' she admonished as she scooped food onto her plate and picked up her chopsticks.

'You forget, Janet. I know your appetite.'

Her eyes flicked up to meet his. The *double entendre* wasn't lost on her and she gave him a shy smile, before lowering her gaze.

'So Leesa called to say hi, did she?'

'She and Hamish are coming over tomorrow night for dinner so, please, make sure you're here promptly at seven-thirty.'

Angus gave a hearty laugh. 'What a fine invitation.'

'As Leesa pointed out, the four of us haven't been together since your return. She's really looking forward to spending time with you.' Janet took another bite of her lemon chicken.

'That's one of the Stevenson sisters,' he pointed out. 'What about the other?'

Janet pretended to be studying her dinner intently, choosing how she should answer that question—if at all. Finally, she looked at him. 'I've seen you every day since you've been back, Angus. You live next door, you work with me.' She shrugged, trying for a display of nonchalance. 'Isn't that enough?'

He gave her a penetrating look which she found difficult to break but finally he nodded. 'Of course. We'll take it slowly.'

'Take what slowly?' she asked with feigned innocence.

'Us. Janet, there's something incredible happening between us. Personally, I don't think we should let it fall by the wayside in case it turns out to be serious.'

'And then what, Angus?' Janet forced her tone to remain calm, although it was far from how she felt.

'And then what?' he repeated. 'Well, I guess we ride it through and see where it takes us. *Carpe diem.* Seize the day.'

'I know what *carpe diem* means, Angus.'

'Then let's go for it, Janet. Let's live life. Let's follow this mutual attraction we feel.'

Janet put a prawn in her mouth and chewed, trying to choose her words carefully.

'I'll think about it,' she said finally, because she wasn't at all sure what she should do. Angus was basically saying that the attraction he felt for her was like no other he'd experienced, yet she knew he still saw it only as an affair—not a lasting lifelong commitment.

'All right. You think about it.' He smiled and Janet quickly looked away, knowing all too well the effect his smile had on her insides. 'Don't keep me waiting too long with your decision,' he chided, and she almost threw a prawn at him.

'You have an enormous ego, Angus O'Donnell.' She smiled at him, glad the awkward moment had passed. 'I'm sorely tempted to cut you down to size.'

'I'd enjoy that,' he whispered seductively, and this time she did toss a prawn at him. It landed on his plate. He picked it up between his chopsticks and held it in front of her mouth.

'I believe, *mademoiselle,* that this belongs to you.' When Janet didn't open her mouth, he moved the prawn closer. Janet swallowed nervously. If she thought the atmosphere before had been uncomfortable, it was nothing compared to now.

Slowly she parted her lips, her tongue darting out briefly to wet them before Angus leaned further forward and placed the prawn in her mouth. Janet's lips closed over the food and chopsticks, her eyes fluttering closed as he slowly withdrew them. She chewed the prawn, her eyes still closed.

The touch of his lips on hers forced her eyes open. She swallowed, then kissed him back—as briefly as he'd kissed her.

'I...' She cleared her throat. 'I am attracted to you, Angus. There's no denying it, but I just...I need some time to sort things out,' she finished quickly. 'You know how women are. We need to analyse everything. Besides, you've only been back a couple of weeks.'

As she said the words Janet found it difficult to believe that so much had happened in such a short time.

'So, for tonight we'll just enjoy each other's company— on a platonic level,' he added quickly as Janet opened her mouth to speak. 'While we wait for you to think and analyse things.'

She returned the smile he gave her. 'Yes. Thank you.'

'Would you like some more rice?' he asked.

That was it? Just like that, he was able to switch topics and bring them back to an even footing.

'Er, yes, please.'

Angus spooned some rice onto her plate and made polite conversation for the rest of the evening.

To her surprise, they did indeed eat all the food he'd ordered, and Janet couldn't remember when she'd enjoyed herself so much. Angus was a charming and funny companion and she cursed herself yet again for falling in love with him. He helped tidy up and stack the dishwasher before they walked to the front door.

'I had a great time tonight,' she said. 'Thanks again for dinner.'

'My pleasure, although I am looking forward to your home cooking tomorrow night.'

Janet smiled as he bent his head to kiss her. It started off as sedate and remote but after a few seconds both of them twined their arms around each other and deepened the kiss.

It was as though they couldn't keep their hands or lips off each other.

Finally they broke apart, their breathing ragged and uneven.

'What time are house calls tomorrow?' Angus asked, and Janet shook her head.

'Don't worry about them this week. I only have one tomorrow, as well as checking up on Mr Campbell in hospital. Go and visit some old friends.'

'I might just do that.' He nodded and Janet knew he'd seen through her attempt at putting some distance between them. He gave her another small kiss, before whispering, 'Think fast, Janet.' Then he opened the door, went outside into the blustery cold night and shut the door quickly behind him.

Reaching into his pocket, he pulled out his keys and unlocked his own door. He threw the keys onto the small table by the door and flicked the light switch. He'd left the heating on low so at least the place wasn't too cold, especially after being in Janet's arms.

Angus walked into the kitchen and went through the motions of making *real* coffee. He'd have to educate Janet and get her off that instant stuff. He raked a hand through his hair as he thought about the kiss they'd just shared.

Janet Stevenson was like no other woman he'd been involved with, and if her answer was that she didn't want to be involved with him, other than reverting back to the sibling relationship they'd shared, he knew he'd have a hard time changing her mind.

Surely she didn't still see him as a brother figure?

'No,' he said out loud. 'Not after *that* kiss.'

He'd have to be patient and take things slowly if he didn't want to blow it. He cared about her too much to intentionally hurt her.

CHAPTER FIVE

JANET hardly slept that night so when she awoke on Saturday morning at eight-thirty, she felt like death warmed up.

Thoughts of Angus, his caresses and his kisses had kept her mind occupied for hours after he'd left. 'Think fast,' he'd said, but Janet was having trouble thinking *straight* at the moment, let alone *fast!*

Stumbling into the shower, she began to wash her hair. By the time she had finished dressing, she felt a bit more human. If she didn't get a move on, she'd be late for Mr Montague.

Negotiating the morning traffic, people on their way to the shopping centres or sporting events, Janet finally pulled into Cyril Montague's driveway and switched the engine off. She was surprised not to see him sitting in the old rocking chair on the front porch. It was Cyril's favourite spot and generally where he spent a good deal of most mornings.

Janet knocked on the door, her medical bag in hand. 'Cyril?' she called out after she'd knocked again. She tried the doorhandle but it was firmly bolted in place. She knocked again, even louder, and called, 'It's Janet Stevenson, Cyril.'

Nothing.

She wandered around to the side of the house and, standing on tiptoe, managed to unlock the gate. Going to the back door, she knocked again.

'Cyril? It's Janet.' Still no answer. She was beginning to get worried. Cyril was seventy-five and a widower. He and his wife had been childhood sweethearts, but three years ago Martha had passed away in her sleep.

Since then Cyril's memory had begun to deteriorate and at his last full examination strong symptoms indicating dementia had been detected.

Janet tried the doorhandle and thankfully this one turned. 'Cyril?' she called out loudly as she walked into the house. There was still no answer and, more importantly, no noise. Janet's feet picked up pace as she began to run from room to room.

'Cyril?' she called as she went through the kitchen into the lounge room. There was no sign of him. She turned and headed for the bedrooms.

'Cyril?' she continued to call as she sprinted up the hallway, opening the doors as she went. When she opened the third bedroom door she came up hard against something. It made her start and a small scream left her lips. A hand came around from the inside of the door and thrust it open.

'What's all the fuss about, girlie? Can't a man enjoy a sleep-in once in a while?' Cyril Montague was completely dressed in his trousers and shirt yet they were all crumpled as though he'd slept in them.

'Oh, Cyril,' Janet almost sobbed as she leaned against the wall for support. 'You scared me—in more ways than one.'

'Well, when you come bursting into a man's house, what do you expect?'

'I'm sorry, Cyril. When you didn't answer the door I began to get worried. I thought something might have happened to you.'

'Like my Martha,' he said wistfully. 'I came home from running an errand for her and there she was, sitting in her favourite chair, knitting needles still in her hands, eyes closed, looking so peaceful.'

'I know,' Janet replied softly with sincerity, and placed

her hand on his shoulder. 'I'm here to give you your check-up so why don't you go back into the bedroom where you'll be comfortable and we'll get it out of the way.'

After checking his blood pressure, listening to his heart and checking his eyes and ears as well as his reflexes, Janet started to pack her bag.

'I'm glad that's out of the way,' Cyril said as he rebuttoned his shirt. 'Alister will be here soon to take me to church.'

'Today's Saturday, Cyril, not Sunday. Alister will be around tomorrow to take you to church. Saturday is the day I come to visit and give you a check-up. Now, how about a cup of tea?' She didn't wait for him to respond. 'I'll put the kettle on while you go and have a wash.'

'Thanks, Janet,' Cyril mumbled, obviously feeling cross with himself for getting the days mixed up.

She stayed an hour with Cyril, making sure he had a good breakfast as the meals-on-wheels people didn't come on weekends, as well as doing a load of washing for him.

'I'm going to apply for someone to come and do some housework for you, Cyril. It will be once a week and they'll just spruce things up a bit. That way, you won't have to worry too much about it.'

'I can manage,' Cyril protested, but he lowered his gaze as he spoke. 'And Leanne comes in now and then to give me a hand. She's a good daughter-in-law, that one.'

'I know.' Janet smiled. 'I've spoken with Alister and Leanne about this and they think it's a good idea. This way you'll have more time to spend in your garden—when the sun's out, of course.'

Cyril thought for a moment. 'When you put it that way, there is a small corner patch of the garden that needs a bit more work doing to it. I want to get it ready for planting some new bulbs for spring.'

'Right, then, the matter's settled. I'll organise the paperwork and someone from domestic cleaning care will be around in a fortnight's time to put the house back in ship-shape condition.'

Cyril started to stutter a bit and Janet continued, 'We'll make sure that either Alister or Leanne are here when the housekeeper arrives. That way you won't be faced with a stranger.'

'That would be good,' he consented. He finished off his breakfast and Janet quickly did the dishes. 'You're a good cook, lass. When are you going to settle down and get married? Have some babies? That's what you need.'

'Soon, Cyril,' Janet answered with a smile. If she settled down any more she'd be buried in the ground but she knew what he meant. 'Now I have to go. I must visit Neville Campbell in hospital and get an update on his condition.'

'Tell him I send my regards,' Cryil said as he walked Janet to the front door. 'Think I'll sit out on the porch for a bit. Most of the morning's gone but it doesn't matter. People still walk by and say hello.'

'Sounds like a good idea to me. I'll be around to see you next Saturday, Cyril. Bye.'

Janet put her bag in the car and reversed out of the drive-way, waving as she left. The traffic had settled down so the drive into Newcastle was completed without frustration.

By the time she'd parked in the doctors' car park and had made her way to ICU, it was almost eleven o'clock. She greeted the nurses and received an update on Mr Campbell's condition.

He had stabilised well and was almost ready for discharge back to a normal ward. He'd managed to keep some food down that morning, which was an excellent sign. Janet walked over to his bed where he was peacefully dozing. She picked up his chart and had a quick scan.

His eyes fluttered open. 'Well, if it isn't my guardian angel,' he whispered with a small smile.

Janet returned his smile. 'It's good to see you looking so much better. You have a lot more colour in your face today and the nurses tell me you've even managed to keep food down. Very good progress indeed.'

'I feel a lot better but still very tired.'

'It's to be expected. Rest is what you need at the moment.'

'Where's Natalie?'

Janet shook her head. 'I haven't seen her. The nurses mentioned that she stayed here last night so perhaps she's popped home to shower and change. I can check with them if you like.'

'No. That sounds like Natalie. Couldn't ask for a better daughter.'

They chatted for a bit longer but Janet could tell Mr Campbell needed some more rest. 'You go back to snoozing and I'll see if I can find Natalie.'

He gave her a nod and Janet walked back to the nurses' station.

'She should be back soon,' one of the nurses replied when Janet asked about Natalie. 'Ah, here she is now.'

Janet turned around to watch Mr Campbell's daughter walk into the ward. She looked refreshed and relaxed—just the type of image her father needed to see right now.

'Hi. Just checking up on Dad?'

'Yes. I hear he's been behaving himself and can be moved out of ICU some time later today. Very good news.'

'He went from strength to strength last night. It was great to see. I'm glad I stayed.'

'I'm sure he's glad you were here as well. I've asked if a dietitian can come and see him after his transfer to the men's ward. Now that he's keeping down food, the hospital will start him on his new diet. Would you mind being there when the dietitian comes? That way, you'll know exactly what's happening.'

'Most certainly,' Natalie nodded. 'I've also discussed it with my husband, and when Dad's discharged from hospital we want him to come and live with us for a while—until he feels comfortable going back to his unit.' She sighed. 'If only we could persuade him to come and live with us permanently, then…' Her voice trailed off.

'Then perhaps you can keep a closer eye on him and hopefully prevent something like this happening again?' Janet asked.

Natalie nodded. 'Something like that. At least, if he was living with us, I could ensure he stuck to the new diet. It's not going to be easy for him.'

'Recovering from another heart attack will be even harder than giving up those doughnuts. He's a reasonable man and I'm sure that once he comprehends things he'll work hard at keeping to his new diet.'

'I hope so. Food has always been his weakness.' Natalie shrugged and smiled. 'What's a girl supposed to do, except love him?'

'Exactly,' Janet replied. 'I presume your father's consultant has spoken to you?'

'Yes. He did a quick ward round this morning and briefly explained what happened and how Dad's heart is healing. He seemed happy with the progress so far.'

'And so he should be. Did you have any questions?'

'No. Not at this stage, but if I do,' she said with emphasis, 'I promise I'll call you.'

'Good.' Janet smiled. 'I'll leave him in your capable hands and get on with the rest of my day.'

'Thanks for everything, Dr Stevenson.'

'You're welcome and, please, call me Janet.'

The two women smiled at each other before Janet said goodbye. With her patients out of the way, that only left organising dinner for this evening. She'd thought about what she'd prepare, wanting everything she made to *really* impress Angus.

Leaving the hospital, she went to the supermarket and started picking up the essential items. She'd decided on potato and leek soup for starters, beef wellington with roast vegetables, a fresh pecan pie and home-made chocolates for dessert.

Then she hurried home to give the place a thorough cleaning and begin preparations. Janet wasn't the type of person to dread house-cleaning as the mindless activity often allowed her time to reflect on matters that were on her mind.

On this occasion, though, all she could think about was Angus. With Hamish and Leesa also here for dinner, did that mean that she and Angus would keep their hands to themselves? Would Angus be open in his attentions to her, letting his brother and her sister know exactly where he stood?

Considering Janet had already spoken to Leesa about her feelings for Angus, he might well have confided in his brother, although, she reasoned, men didn't usually do that kind of thing.

Taking a deep breath as she refreshed the towels in the bathroom, Janet knew that no amount of speculation was going to help her. With most of the food prepared and ready to go, she rushed to her bedroom and threw open the wardrobe door.

'Something casual yet elegant. Comfortable yet alluring.' She pulled out one outfit after another and discarded them onto the bed with a flick of her wrist. 'Don't look as though you're trying too hard,' Janet told her reflection as yet another outfit landed on the bed.

She turned and looked at the mess behind her. 'See what you've done to me, Angus O'Donnell? You've turned me from a calm and rational woman into a blithering nincompoop who spends hours wondering what to wear to a dinner party in her own home!'

The phone extension in her bedroom shrilled to life, startling Janet. She quickly snatched the receiver from its cradle. 'Hello? Dr Stevenson here.'

'Janet.' Angus's voice smoothed over her. Her knees gave way and she collapsed onto the bed, her breathing rate increasing and her cheeks growing warm with embarrassment. It's all right, she told herself. He can't see or hear what you've been saying. Relax.

'Yes, Angus,' she said with a bit more severity than she'd intended.

'I wanted to pick up a few bottles of wine and need to know what delicious, mouth-watering treats you've prepared for us this evening.'

'Beef. Don't worry about the wine—Leesa's organising that.'

'Perhaps I can bring some chocolates to go with coffee?'

'I've made some myself and they're chilling in the fridge. Really, Angus. Just bring yourself.'

'Are you all right? You sound a bit frazzled.'

'Everything's fine. I'm just putting the final touches on things.' She fingered an embroidered white silk blouse which had landed on top of the heap.

'Can I give you a hand? I'm free at the moment.'

'No,' she said a little too quickly. 'Actually, I'm just deciding what to wear.'

'Now, *there* I can help you,' he responded, and she could hear the smile in his voice. 'I'll be right over.'

'No! Angus, it's all—' but she was too late. Angus had hung up. Moments later he was knocking on her front door.

'Come on, Janet. I know you're in there.'

Janet opened the door and let him in. 'It's really not necessary, Angus.' She turned away from him, not wanting to make eye contact. At the mere sound of his voice the

butterflies that seemed to be living permanently in her
stomach took flight. Now the smell of his aftershave was
mingling with her senses, causing her to fall under his spell
once again. 'I'm more than capable of finding something
to wear. Besides, Leesa and Hamish will be here in another
half-hour or so and I need to finish things off.' She walked
into the kitchen and motioned to the things around her.

'That's why I'm here,' he said good-naturedly and
walked over to her. Placing one hand under her chin, Angus
lifted her head so their eyes could meet. 'To tell the truth,
Janet, I simply wanted an excuse to come over and do
this...' He bent his head and placed his lips firmly and
seductively on hers. 'Before our siblings arrive,' he finished
softly. 'I haven't been able to get you out of my mind all
day.'

Janet didn't know what to do. She knew Angus was attracted to her but she hadn't expected to hear a confession
such as that. It was, she supposed, what every woman
wanted to hear from the man they'd fallen in love with, but
Janet realised that she was just that—every woman. Angus
probably had a different woman in each country or town
he'd worked in over the past eight years.

What right did she have to think that she might be different? Sure, they were old friends and had strong family
connections, but what if things didn't work out? If there
was one thing Janet had realised in the last few weeks, it
was that regardless of her feelings for Angus, he was still
going to up and leave at the end of his six-month contract.
Any hope she had of changing his mind seemed remote
and, besides, she refused to play mind games with a man
who would no doubt leave her hurt and alone in the end.

He must have read the confusion in her eyes because he
took a step back and dropped his hand. The smile on his
face was a casual one—a friendly one—and Janet couldn't
resist, but smiled back.

She looked at him properly for the first time since he'd walked in. He was dressed in boots, black denim jeans and a chambray shirt that was open at the neck. The heating throughout her home provided ample warmth for him not to need a jacket.

He allowed her inspection of him with a raised eyebrow, before subjecting her to a similar appraisal. The warmth of his gaze as it flowed over her body brought the bubbling desire back to the surface.

When he spoke, his tone was friendly and teasing. 'You do need to change, Cinderella. This outfit...' he gestured to the old track pants and T-shirt she usually wore when she cleaned her house '...will never do for tonight's event. Come. Let us away to the secret chamber where I, your fairy god...ah...person, will transform you into the beautiful princess.'

With that, he took her by the hand and tugged her down the hallway to her bedroom. Walking into the room, he stopped, looking with astonishment at the pile of clothes on the bed.

'Just as well I stopped by,' he drawled as he walked over and picked up a few coat hangers, before returning them to the wardrobe. 'Looks as though Cindy dear can't make up her mind what to wear.'

Janet gathered the clothes off the bed and hung them back up as Angus sat down, watching her intently. The fact that he was sitting on her bed was causing such a mixture of emotions in her that she couldn't think straight. She should tell him to go and come back when Leesa and Hamish had arrived. Yes, that's what she should do, she thought as she hung the last of the clothes back up.

Turning around to ask him to leave, Janet was surprised to see he'd left the bed and had crossed over to the chest of drawers.

'Do you have a cream-coloured top?'

His request puzzled Janet for a moment but she pulled open the middle drawer and rummaged around, before extracting a V-neck knit. She held it up against herself for inspection, and to her delight saw his Adam's apple work its way up and down his throat as he swallowed convulsively.

'Perfect.' His voice was deep and sensual. 'Wear that with a pair of denim Levis and you'll look…incredible.' He breathed the last word and Janet lowered her arms, the cream knit sliding from her fingers as their gazes locked.

Slowly, Angus closed the distance between them, bringing his hands up to cup her face. 'Don't get me wrong. You're beautiful, Janet. Even in the old clothes you're wearing now, you're still stunning.' With that, he lowered his head and claimed her lips ever so gently with his.

Her eyes fluttered closed as she allowed him to once more weave his magic throughout her being. Tantalisingly, he parted her lips with his tongue, slipping it just inside her mouth before running it the length of her lower lip.

'Angus,' she whispered.

'Shh,' he replied. 'Get dressed. I'll wait in the lounge room.' With that, he turned and walked out only moments before Janet collapsed onto the bed, her entire body alive with burning desire.

She lay there for a few more minutes, willing her traitorous body to return to normal. When she thought she could stand, Janet changed her clothes. It was oddly sensual, putting on the garments Angus had chosen. Unable to decide what to do with her hair, she applied a small amount of make-up while she deliberated.

Upon hearing the doorbell, the decision was easily reached. She tugged the band out which had held it back in a careless ponytail while she'd cleaned the house and began to brush it. The reddish highlights shone brilliantly and, satisfied with her reflection, she went to meet her family.

'You're a bit early,' she accused Leesa as she gave her sister a hug.

'It's Hamish's fault.' Leesa walked through to the kitchen, carrying two bottles of wine. 'We came in his car and you know what a speed freak he is,' Leesa joked, all of them knowing full well that it wasn't true. Hamish drove with the utmost care and precision—exactly the way he appeared to do everything else in his life.

Janet accepted a brotherly hug and peck on the cheek from Hamish as he handed her the latest medical journal.

'There's a good article in there on community medicine—a topic I know is close to your heart, Janet.'

'You're such a romantic, Hamish.' Angus laughed. 'Usually when you're dining at someone else's house, it's protocol to arrive with wine, chocolates or flowers—even all three on occasions—but not my brother.'

Leesa joined in the laughter as she walked into the lounge room and sat down. 'It's just Hamish's way,' she defended him, her love for him shining brightly in her eyes.

'Don't listen to them, Hamish. It's the perfect thing to bring. Leesa brought the wine and I have plenty of chocolates and flowers, but this article will be interesting. Thank you.'

They all sat down in the lounge room and relaxed for a while before Janet went to put the finishing touches to the meal.

Two hours later, she had no idea why she'd thought things might be a little awkward this evening. Angus was delighting them all with stories of his travels while Leesa and Hamish passed on anecdotes on hospital life. The food was lavishly complimented, especially by Angus, giving Janet a tingling sensation of accomplishment.

While they were enjoying coffee with Janet's home-made chocolates, Leesa managed inadvertently to ruin her sister's evening.

'So, what's next?' she asked Angus after he'd finished telling them about a close encounter in India with a snake charmer—*and* the snake! 'Rome? Paris? London?'

Angus shrugged, his eyes not meeting Janet's. 'Been there, done that. Actually, I thought I'd stay in the southern hemisphere for a while. I have an old colleague in New Zealand who's asked me to speak at a conference in just over four weeks' time on some non-invasive techniques I used in the Lake District some years ago. I'll see what eventuates when I catch up with him. Besides, there's some other business I need to attend to while I'm there.' He looked at Hamish when he spoke and his older brother gave him a knowing nod.

Again, Janet realised there was something else going on and her curiosity was definitely piqued, but the fact remained that Angus was still planning on leaving at the end of his six-month contract. It made her mouth go dry and she swallowed. He would leave and she'd be alone.

The conversation seemed to flow over her and tears started to well in her eyes. She quickly excused herself, saying she'd make some more coffee.

Moments later Leesa came into the kitchen and placed a hand on Janet's shoulder. 'I guess you were right,' she said. 'He isn't going to stay. I'm sorry if it hurt you to hear his answer but at least this way we know for sure that he won't even *consider* staying. So, what are you going to do?'

Janet shook her head and looked at her sister. 'Keep my distance.' She took a deep breath and forced herself to relax. 'There's nothing else I *can* do. Angus will remain my business associate and friend but that's all.'

'These O'Donnell men need their heads read,' Leesa said gruffly, and thumped her fist down on the bench. 'They have two incredible Stevenson women before them and neither of them realise what they're missing. I wish Mary would come back. She'd knock some sense into her sons.'

Leesa's comment received a smile from Janet. 'Yes, she would.'

'Should I give her a call?' Leesa enquired, and the two women laughed, the sombre mood broken. 'Come on. I promised Hamish one more cup of coffee before we really must be going. Although it's Saturday, we still have ward round first thing tomorrow morning and then I have a pile of paperwork to get through.'

'The life of a registrar…' Janet said, and shook her head. 'Thanks for helping me through, sis.'

'That's what I'm here for,' Leesa replied.

True to her word, Leesa ushered Hamish out of the house after one more cup of coffee. 'Time we left Janet in peace,' Leesa told Angus when it appeared he was going to stay.

'I'll just help her clean up a bit, before sending her off to bed. It was good to see you again, Leesa.' Angus gave her a brotherly hug. 'You've changed a lot in eight years. No longer the uncoordinated medical student but a beautiful and intelligent orthopaedic registrar. What do you say, Hamish? Hasn't our little Leesa blossomed into the most stunning of women?'

Hamish didn't look twice at Leesa and merely shrugged at his brother's comment. 'There's more to a woman than looks, Angus. If Leesa continues the way she's going, she'll score very well on her final orthopaedic exams. That should be her main focus for the next few years.' With that, Hamish thanked Janet for the delicious meal, shook his brother's hand and ushered Leesa to the car.

After they'd gone, Janet turned to Angus. She was starting to shiver a bit now and just wanted to get inside— alone—to tidy things up. 'You go on home, Angus. There isn't that much to do.'

'No. I insist on helping you.' He walked into her house,

leaving her to either freeze or follow. Janet followed and shut the door with more force than necessary. Why wouldn't the man take a hint?

She found him carrying the empty coffee cups into the kitchen. Wordlessly, Janet took them from him, stacked them into the dishwasher, rearranged a few other dishes and, considering it was full, switched it on. Angus took a cloth and wiped the table in the lounge room, before returning.

'That's about it.' She motioned to the clean kitchen. 'Thanks for your help.'

Angus curled his arm about her waist and drew her closer. 'It was my pleasure,' he drawled as he lowered his head to claim her lips. Janet kissed him back but tried to temper her response. 'It's been terrible, trying to keep my hands off you for the past few hours, but I had no idea whether you wanted Hamish and Leesa to know about us.'

She eased out of his grasp and stood looking at him. 'What us?' she asked quietly. 'There is no *us,* Angus.' She shook her head sadly.

He frowned. 'What about the feelings we have for each other?'

'Exactly. What about them, Angus? What feelings *do* you have for me?'

He faltered for a moment, before saying carefully, 'There's an undeniably strong attraction between us, Janet. One that has caught us both off guard.'

'Agreed.'

'We owe it to ourselves to pursue that attraction. See where it takes us. It could be the most incredible experience of our lives.'

'Agreed—but what happens after that?'

'*After?*' His frown deepened.

'Yes, Angus. After!' Janet's tone held such urgency she

thought it might frighten him off for good. 'Going to bed isn't going to solve anything.'

'But at least we'll find out if we're compatible in that quarter.'

'I *know* we'll be compatible in that quarter. I have no doubt that sex with you would be out of this world, but what happens after?' When he didn't answer she pressed on carefully. 'You know I'm like this, Angus. I'm not a spontaneous person. I've always planned every little step I've ever taken to the nth degree. This is who I am, Angus. I refuse to jump into bed with you and have a wild and wonderful six-month affair before you up and leave me for the next woman in…New Zealand.'

'So that's the real problem,' he said, nodding. 'The fact that I won't be around for longer than six months.'

'I'm the one who'll be staying behind. In the same job, in the same house, having to pick up the pieces of my life while you just move on and forget anyone who's ever meant anything to you.' Her voice broke on a sob and she turned her back to him.

'Janet.' Angus placed a hand on Janet's shoulder to turn her around but she stepped away. 'Janet, I can't talk to your back. Please look at me.'

Taking a deep breath, she faced him, her eyes desperately trying to veil the hurt she was already feeling.

'The first year after I left Newcastle, I worked for a woman in the States. We grew very close. When my six months was up she begged me to stay. I did, and two months later everything was over—including my job. I had very little money and nowhere to live as that was part and parcel of my job.'

'You were just starting out then,' she reasoned. 'You were only thirty. You have so much experience behind you now.'

He shook his head. 'I can't stay. It just doesn't work.' He spread his arms wide.

'You're scared,' Janet said, the realisation knocking her for six. 'You're completely scared of being hurt again so, instead, you hurt others around you.' She nodded slowly, surprised she hadn't thought about this before. 'It all makes sense. You use the excuse of being free and travelling the globe as a shield against getting hurt.'

'It's not like that at all.' He looked down at the ground and Janet waited for him to speak. Slowly he raised his head and said quietly, 'After that incident I just mentioned, I hooked up with a…' He hesitated and then, as though making a decision, continued, 'Particular company in the States and part of my agreement with them is that I move on every six months.'

'What? Who?'

'I know it sounds strange but it's all I can tell you at the moment. I'm sorry, Janet, it's confidential.'

Janet slumped down into a chair and absorbed his words. 'You aren't involved in anything illegal, are you?'

'No. I promise you, it's quite the opposite.' He crouched down in front of her and took her hands in his. 'What about us, Janet? Where do we go from here?'

Janet sighed, feeling drained. 'Where do *you* want to go? I can guess but why don't you spell it out for me?'

'I want to spend our rainy evenings together and enjoy the warmer days when they arrive. I want to enjoy your home cooking as well as taking you out to dinner. I want to talk with you, laugh with you and just relax with you. I want to touch you as you've never been touched before. I want to kiss you as you've never been kissed before. I want to make love to you and hold you until the sun comes up.'

He claimed her lips in a searing kiss. Janet was helpless against his onslaught and instinctively leaned towards him, kissing him back with all the love she possessed.

When he finally broke free she saw a gleam of triumph in his eyes. Feeling hurt, she brushed him aside and stood up, putting some distance between them.

'I'm glad you want all those things, Angus. I would like them too, only…' It was her turn to hesitate. 'I want more. I want what most women want. Marriage—children—*permanence.*' She was silent for a moment, before continuing, 'We'll always be friends, Angus. Regardless of this attraction between us, we'll always have that. I think we should keep it that way.'

He was silent and she could almost feel his internal struggle. Finally he said, 'Friends it is, then.' He bent and kissed her cheek. 'Thanks for the meal, Janet. Your cooking, as usual, was mouth-wateringly delicious. Don't come to the door. I'll see myself out.'

He turned and walked down the hallway, Janet's eyes following his progress until he was out of sight. She heard the front door open and then close with a resounding thud.

It took a few minutes for everything to sink in. She switched off the lights on her way to the bathroom where she undressed and prepared for bed. Only when she was snuggled up against the pillow and duvet did she give way to her tears, crying herself to sleep.

CHAPTER SIX

ON MONDAY morning, Janet arrived at work early. She hadn't heard any sounds from Angus's house and she'd told herself she couldn't care less.

'Concentrate on work.' She sat down behind her desk. 'Yesterday was for wallowing in self-pity but today it's over. You and Angus are just friends. *Friends.*' She picked up her clinic list and sighed. A few of the patients from last Friday's clinic had made new appointments due to the emergency with Mr Campbell, obviously not comfortable seeing 'the new doctor'.

She opened her diary and read her list of things to do. In three weeks' time she was due to speak at the university on the topic of community medicine. It was her first speaking appointment and she hoped it wouldn't be the last. There was a great shortage of general knowledge in most communities and she had a real passion to get something stable and informative up and running.

One of the ways she'd planned to do this was by speaking to final-year medical students and interns. Thankfully, one of her old friends from medical school was a part-time lecturer and had a bit of clout with the university. He'd pulled some strings and had managed to get Janet this first speaking engagement. If she did well, they would be asking her back on a more permanent basis.

She had little contact with Angus that morning except when she literally bumped into him in the kitchen.

'Coffee-time,' he said from behind her as she closed the fridge, milk in hand. The carton slipped out of her fingers and Angus quickly reached around her body to catch it before it landed on the floor.

The immediate contact of his arm as it brushed against hers caused shooting spasms of desire to rip through her. She gasped as though he'd scalded her and quickly stepped away. He must have seen the reaction in her eyes because he placed the milk on the bench and shoved his hands into his trouser pockets.

'It's going to be harder than we thought,' he murmured, and smiled that cute little boy smile she loved so much.

'We're strong,' she commented, schooling her thoughts and concentrating on making coffee.

There was silence for an awkward moment before he volunteered, 'I've called the pathology department at the hospital and Mr Davies not only turned up for his appointment but allowed the tests to proceed without complaint.'

'Good. I think we scared him enough for him to start taking this seriously.'

'They'll ring the results through as soon as they have them.'

'Good,' she repeated. With her coffee made, she picked up her cup. 'Back to the grindstone.'

In her office, she took five good steadying breaths and a sip of her coffee, before sitting down and picking up the telephone. She dialled the office number for Cyril Montague's son Alister.

'It's Janet Stevenson here, Alister. Have I caught you at a bad time?'

'No. Things are quiet here. I've been expecting your call.'

'How was your father yesterday when you took him to church?'

'Confused. He wasn't dressed when I arrived and didn't know what day it was. I managed to get him dressed and off to church. Afterwards, we brought him home with us for lunch. As we had a bit of sunshine, he went outside with the two boys and was watching them play football. The next thing we knew he'd gone. Just like that. Neither of the boys had seen him walk off and thought he'd simply come back inside. We found him down at the corner shops. I didn't know whether to yell at him or hug him, I was so relieved to find him.'

'What was he doing there?' Janet asked calmly, but Alister's words were only confirming what she'd already suspected.

'That's the strange part. He said that Mum had asked him to come down and buy some sweets for her. Caramel chocolates were her favourite and, sure enough, he had a bag of them in his hand but no money to pay for them. The shop assistant knew he was my father and was trying to ring our house when we walked in.' Alister sighed. 'Poor Dad had no idea what the confusion was all about.'

'He was very vague when I called around on Saturday as well—had his days mixed up.'

'Does it mean anything?'

'Yes, Alister, I'm afraid it does. It looks as though your father is in the first stages of dementia.'

'Isn't that just another term for old age?'

'No, unfortunately, it's not.' Janet took a deep breath. 'Dementia is a syndrome of failing memory and progressive loss of intellectual power due to a continuing degenerative disease of the brain. Basically, Alister, dementia causes the patient to regress.

'When a baby is first born, it can't think for itself. It needs to have everything done for it. Being fed, having nappies changed, and so on. Then the child learns to crawl, walk, talk, eat and so the skills progress. With dementia, it goes backwards. The confusion your father is experiencing is one of the first signs exhibited by dementia sufferers. He'll start wandering off—which he did yesterday. He'll lose his direction—even the house he's lived in for the past fifty years will turn into a maze. He'll experience loss of mechanical function—doing things in the wrong order. For example, if he's making a cup of tea, he might put the tea into the kettle and then pour the water down the sink. Loss of control of bodily function. The sense of balance goes and in most cases the patient will do themselves an injury which requires hospitalisation.'

'Like falling and breaking their leg or hip?' Alister asked.

'Exactly. I think it might be a good idea for me to arrange a time to come and speak with you and Leanne about what to do next.'

'What *should* we do next?'

'Is it possible he could move in with you? I know how Cyril feels about nursing homes and to suggest one to him would be disastrous at this stage, but it will be a necessity in the longer term. Just the suggestion that someone comes in and cleans his house was a big step for him to agree to.'

'He'd be more than welcome to come and live with us as we have a spare room. I mentioned it when Mum died three years ago but he refused. He loves that house. It's where he first brought his bride home to over fifty years ago. He says the house makes him feel closer to her memory.'

'He needs to hold onto his memories for as long as he can,' Janet replied. 'I'll ask the district nurse to visit him twice a week instead of weekly. The meals-on-wheels people come every week-day and the cleaning service can be organised for once or twice weekly.'

'Are these cleaners…?' Alister hesitated. 'Are they sensitive to this type of person?'

Janet smiled. 'Yes. They're specifically for the aged who are still living at home but can't quite cope with the cleaning side of things.'

'And the cost?'

'The scheme is partly government funded so the cost isn't too great.'

'It doesn't matter,' Alister assured her quickly. 'We can cover it if it means Dad's happy.'

'I can understand why he doesn't want to leave,' Janet said carefully. 'Unfortunately, Alister, the dementia will attack his memories along with everything else. I can't imagine what the street would be like without Cyril sitting on his front porch, watching the world go by.'

'One of his favourite spots,' Alister commented.

'Right. I'll organise the domestic cleaners and tell you when they're coming around—probably in a fortnight because of the red tape involved. I know you or Leanne will want to be there when the person arrives.'

'Yes, we will. Is there any treatment for the dementia?'

'It varies from person to person. To begin with, I'd like your father to have an EEG some time in the next few weeks. EEG,' she continued before he could ask the obvious question, 'stands for electroencephalogram. It's when electrodes are placed at certain points on the scalp. Tracings are made on a long piece of graph paper and form patterns which can then be read by the specialist. It's the abnormal tracings that we're looking for in this instance. They'll show the level of disturbance so the agitation and attacks of violence which are common in dementia patients can be treated with the right medication. If he has one done now, as the disease progresses, we can monitor the changes in neural patterns.'

'Where would he have it done?'

'Up at the hospital. I can give you the contact number so you can make the appointment at a time convenient to both you and your father. If you ring the date and time through to Karen, I'll arrange for the referral letter to be sent to the hospital—save you a trip in here.'

'OK. I'll do that straight away.'

Janet gave Alister the contact number and then said,
'Perhaps, after he's had the scan, I can come and speak
with you and Leanne, but in the meantime if either of you
have any questions you give me a call.'

'Will do, Janet, and thanks.'

'Not a problem, Alister. Take care.' She rang off and
picked up her pen. She made some notes on Cyril
Montague's file and filled in the paperwork for the cleaning
service. Next she wrote a small note to Karen, giving in-
structions and information so her receptionist was appraised
of the situation.

The rest of the afternoon flowed without complication
and, amazingly, Janet finished on time. 'See what happens
when you have another doctor around to help carry the
load,' she told herself as she tidied her desk.

'Talking to yourself is the first sign of insanity,' Angus
said from her open doorway. He had his coat on and his
briefcase in hand. 'Can I walk you home?'

'Uh...sure. Why not, considering we're both walking the
same way?' She put her coat on and picked up her bag and
briefcase.

He waited while she switched off her light and walked
out to Reception. 'Goodnight, Karen,' she said, and Angus
echoed her words as they left the receptionist to lock up.

'Chilly night,' Angus commented.

'Yes,' came Janet's monosyllabic reply.

They walked on.

'The sun is setting quite early. It's completely gone by
six o'clock at the moment.'

'Yes,' she repeated.

They walked on.

'Any complications this afternoon?' Angus tried again.

'None.'

They walked on.

'Janet,' Angus said finally, and stopped walking. She stopped a few paces ahead and turned to look at him.

'Yes?'

'This is ridiculous. Surely we should be able to carry on a conversation that consists of more than yes and no replies.'

She turned away and started walking slowly. 'I didn't say no, I answered "none" to your question.'

'Stop being pedantic,' he said as he caught up with her.

'Angus, I'm starting to get cold and I'd like to get home where it's nice and warm.'

'Will you talk to me then?'

'It depends. What would you want to talk about?'

'Do I have to submit a list in advance?' She could tell he was trying to be funny but it wasn't going to work. Not this time.

'Perhaps it would be better if you did. There are some topics I think we should no longer discuss.'

'Namely our relationship.'

'Top of the list for topics to avoid,' she agreed.

They walked on. Janet had increased her pace, eager to get to her front door. They rounded the corner of their street and she crossed the road, heading for her gate.

'What about family?'

'Sure, we can discuss our families, but I know how agitated you get when you even think about your mother, let alone talk about her, so I thought that *you* would veto that subject.'

'Hamish and Leesa?' he asked hopefully.

'What's there to discuss?' Janet walked down her front path, Angus hard on her heels. 'How Leesa can put up with your brother's lack of observation? Why she keeps holding onto the dream that Hamish will one day turn around and see her for the beautiful swan she's become?' She shook her head as she fished out her keys and unlocked her door.

'I don't know if there's much else to discuss regarding those two. They're perfectly suited. Everyone can see it—except your brother. And if you ask me, the defect is genetic because it appears to run in your family.' With that, she opened her door and said, 'Goodnight, Angus. Thank you for walking me home.' Then she shut the door in his face.

On Tuesday, Angus walked into her consulting room just before lunch and handed her a piece of paper.

Janet read the pathology result on Mr Davies's tests.

'Have you notified him with these results yet?'

'Not yet. This is a part of our job that I don't like—giving patients bad news. Mr Davies will need to have a widespread excision on his arm. He'll be in hospital and, depending on those results, may in the longer term need radio- or chemotherapy.'

'One thing we know for sure, Angus. He'll take this news better from you than me.'

Angus looked at her for a long moment, then stood up. 'True.' When he reached the door, Janet called his name.

'Did you *really* come in here to discuss Mr Davies?'

'Why else would I be here?' He looked at her with an innocent expression on his face.

'Indeed.' She frowned. Karen buzzed to ask if she could squeeze another patient in before lunch, and when Janet looked at the door again Angus was gone.

Out in the hallway, Angus smiled secretly to himself as he walked to his office. Janet was getting to know him a little too well if she suspected him of entering her room under false pretences.

He'd been looking for an excuse to interrupt her all morning. He'd just wanted to see her—that was all. Then, once he'd found himself in there, he hadn't wanted to leave. He'd wanted to ask her out to dinner tonight so they could talk more about their relationship—or lack thereof—but he was sure she would decline. Friends, she'd suggested. Well, friends could go out to dinner, couldn't they?

He wanted to ask her about that comment she'd thrown at him the previous evening—right before slamming the door in his face. That both he and Hamish shared a genetic defect.

As far as he was concerned, the only thing besides the same parents he shared with Hamish, was the O'Donnell dark hair and blue eyes.

Other than that, they were like chalk and cheese. That wasn't to say they didn't get along well because Angus knew they accepted each other for who they were.

He shook his head as he walked over to his desk. Nope. He couldn't think of a genetic defect at all!

Mr Davies accepted the news with a surprising calmness and willingly co-operated with his oncologist, Dr Catherine Hamilton.

'So he took the news relatively well?' Janet asked the following day when Angus related the events of his meeting with Mr Davies.

'Yes. He seems more than willing to co-operate with Dr Hamilton. The seriousness of his situation has finally sunk in.'

'That's such good news. It was a battle every time he came in just to get him to tell me what was wrong.' She looked across to where Angus sat opposite her, the desk separating them. 'Thank you for making him feel comfortable.'

'The only thing I've done differently from you is to be the opposite sex, something which I had no say in at all.'

'Then I'll thank your parents instead.' Janet smiled. 'Seriously, at least Mr Davies is being treated.'

'Another satisfied customer,' Angus commented as he stood up.

'Precisely. Thanks for keeping me up to date.'

'No problem.' He smiled his winning smile and Janet felt herself begin to melt. Their gazes held for a moment and the smile started to vanish from his face, his eyes growing dark with desire.

'Janet?' Karen's voice came through the intercom.

Janet broke eye contact, her body trembling slightly at his visual caress. 'Yes?' she said, after depressing the button.

'There's a call from the university for you on line two.'

'Thanks. Put it through.' The phone rang and Janet picked the receiver up. Angus, to her chagrin, didn't leave but listened unashamedly to her end of the conversation.

'I have them ready to post now,' Janet said, desperately trying to block him out of her mind and concentrate on her caller. 'Yes, I'm looking forward to it, too.' She paused. 'Thanks for calling. I'll see you then.'

'Doing some lecturing?' he asked as she hung up.

Janet nodded. 'In a few weeks' time.'

'Why didn't you say anything?'

'Didn't think it was important.'

'What topic are you speaking on?'

'How doctors like us can raise the awareness of community medicine.'

'Oh.' He frowned for a moment then smiled again. 'Good for you.'

'Something wrong?' Janet tried not to let her spirits plummet at his not-so-favourable response.

'No. Nothing's wrong. I guess I just expected you to say something else.'

'Like a breakthrough in cancer treatments? Sorry, Angus. I'm just a suburban GP. My practice revolves around the community and raising awareness in that community about general health issues is in great need of improvement.'

'I agree with you,' he said, his hands held up in defence.

'Sorry.' She smiled. 'It's pet topic of mine, which is why I applied to speak at the university.'

'And, no doubt, you'll do brilliantly. Mind if I tag along?'

'I'd prefer you not to,' Janet said, not at all sure whether she wanted him sitting in the audience while she spoke. He had such a disturbing effect on her equilibrium that she might not be able to concentrate on her speech.

'Think about it,' he offered, not accepting her answer, and took a step towards the door. 'I'd better get back to work. Don't want to upset the boss.'

'But you're talking to the boss,' Janet said.

'You? You think you're the boss in this practice?' He shook his head, a twinkle in his eye. 'You may pay the wages, Janet, but the true boss is Karen. She runs this place like clockwork, and if I don't get back to the consulting room before my next patient arrives she'll have my head.'

'She is a great practice manager, isn't she?'

'The greatest. There are some practices that would pay a king's ransom to steal her away from you.'

'Shh,' Janet laughed and placed a finger over her lips. 'Don't you dare tell Karen. I don't want her jet-setting around the world as well. It's bad enough that I'll be losing you in a few months' time, let alone ''the boss''!'

Angus sobered. 'Will it be bad to lose me?'

'Of course. You're a fantastic doctor, Angus.'

He looked at her for a few more seconds, before nodding. They both heard the tinkle of the front doorbell, indicating that another patient had arrived.

'Better get going,' Janet suggested, and with that, he left her room.

On Saturday, Janet took Angus with her to visit Cyril Montague. There had been no change in his condition since the previous week, except that he kept forgetting Angus's name.

'It's all right,' Janet told him as he continued to get frustrated. 'Try not to let the frustration get to you. Just relax and enjoy your cup of tea. As far as Angus is concerned, I doubt if he bothers what you called him.'

'So long as it's complimentary,' Angus added, and Cyril chuckled.

'This one's all right, lassie,' he said in a stage whisper, although Angus could hear him quite clearly. 'How about settling down with him and having some babies?'

Janet kept her gaze fixed firmly on her cup as she said, 'Good idea, Cyril. I might just do that.'

'I should charge a matchmaking fee.' He chuckled again. Janet could feel a tell-tale blush heating her face but refused to look at Angus. She was afraid he would read the truth in her eyes—that she wanted to do just that *with him* and no one else.

A fortnight later, Cyril had a clean house and increased district-nursing care. He was happy and coping well for the time being. His EEG had confirmed her suspicions but at least now they could formulate a treatment plan. Leanne and Alister Montague were open to any help they could give to Cyril and Janet knew that, regardless of what happened to Cyril and when, he would be loved and cared for.

On Monday, Hannah Kellerman had brought her healthy and happy son back to see Janet.

'He looks good. What can I do for you today?' Janet asked as she smiled at the single mother.

'Immunisations. I know he's a bit late, but with him not being well before—'

'Say no more,' Janet interrupted. 'Do you have his book?'

Hannah handed over the book containing Sam's immunisation details and Janet filled in the paperwork, before preparing the injections. 'He has his diphtheria, tetanus and pertussis injection in one leg and his HIB injection in the other. HIB stands for *Haemophilus influenzae*, type B, just in case you've forgotten it since his injections a few months ago,' Janet informed Hannah as she finished drawing up the shot and replacing the protective cap over the needle.

'Doesn't he also have an oral one?'

'Yes. I'll give that to him first before we jab the poor little fellow with needles.' Janet organised the oral vaccine. She put some sugar onto the end of a spatula and added the medication. 'This is for poliomyelitis,' she told Hannah as she placed the spatula sugar side down on Sam's tongue. 'It's rather bitter so the little bit of sugar helps it go down.'

'Just like the Mary Poppins song.' Hannah laughed.

'Exactly. Right. If you'd like to unbutton his stretchsuit and get his legs out, then lie him down on the examination couch, we'll get these injections over and done with.'

Soon little Sam's wails could be heard throughout the entire clinic. 'Shh,' Janet said as she packed things up while Hannah dressed her son.

'You were a very good boy.' Janet gave his forehead a kiss. 'He may be a little bit grumpy for the next few hours. He shouldn't get a temperature, but if he does, give him infant paracetamol four-hourly. Sometimes they do and sometimes they don't. It depends on the child and even then the temperature is usually very mild. If it's otherwise and it doesn't break within eight hours, call me immediately.'

'Thanks.' Hannah gave Sam his favourite toy which he took and immediately put into his mouth, his cries starting to subside. 'Oh, surely you're not hungry *again*?' she groaned.

Janet smiled. 'A feed might settle him down, although he appears to be coping fine now.' She wiped a tear from his cheek.

Hannah hesitated for a moment.

'Was there something else?'

'Well, actually…I was thinking about those mothers' groups you've mentioned before.'

'Yes. The parents' support group?'

'Yes. I guess it would be…kind of nice to speak to someone about things. I don't like to bother you all the time,' she finished quickly.

Janet pulled a brochure from her drawer and handed it to Hannah. 'I don't mind you bothering me at all, but this support group will provide more practical advice. Remember, Hannah, I'm not a mother. The main aim of these groups are to help people like yourself who are basically coping by themselves. Even just getting together and having a cup of coffee with someone who's in a similar predicament can go a long way to helping.

'It makes you realise you're not the only person experiencing the constant feeding, or crying, or the sleepless nights or whatever. It makes you feel…normal and *that* goes a long way to improving your self-esteem. You're a good mother, Hannah. You take very good care of Sam and taking this step—especially when I know how hard it is for you to ask for help—is another indication of how much you care for your son.'

Hannah blushed at Janet's words. 'Thank you. It means a lot to hear you say that.'

'It's the truth. Read the information and, please, give them a call. It's worth a try and I guarantee you'll meet some very interesting people.'

'OK. Well, we'd better be going so you can get on with your clinic,' Hannah said, and shoved the brochure and Sam's immunisation record into the baby bag, before hoisting it over her shoulder. Sam was still chewing on his toy.

'You might want to check his gums, too,' Janet suggested as she held the door open for them. 'It looks as though he's ready to cut some teeth.' She brushed her finger across Sam's hot, pink cheek and smiled at Hannah. 'Take care.'

After closing the door, Janet wrote up the notes, thankful that Hannah had decided to seek more help. Raising a child alone wasn't easy and Janet admired the women who toughed it out to give their children the best they could give.

She sighed, her longing for a child of her own increasing. Marriage and children. Yes, she wanted it all and she wanted it with only one man.

Pulling herself away from those thoughts, as they only upset her, she checked her diary. She needed to address the issue of finding a permanent partner. When should she advertise? She was tempted to offer the job to Angus one last time in the hope that he'd accept but he'd made himself quite clear on that point.

In just over one week's time he would be off to New Zealand to speak at a conference. He'd also mentioned he had other business to attend to while he was in New Zealand. Did it have anything to do with the mysterious company he worked for? She shook her head. There was a huge slice of the jig-saw puzzle missing, but one thing she knew for certain—if he left her, her heart would go with him.

Part of her wanted to hold him—prevent him from making the trip that would eventually take him away from her for ever. The sensible part of her knew it would be foolhardy to attempt. Angus had been honest and forthright from the beginning. As she wrote out the third draft for the advertisement, she felt she was being slightly deceitful to her feelings for Angus. How could she do this when perhaps…perhaps if she told him she loved him, he would reconsider?

Yet, if she told him the truth, it would definitely give him more power over her. During the past weeks they'd only seen each other either in the hallways or in the kitchen, making coffee. She'd cancelled the weekly practice meeting she and Karen usually had because she couldn't be around Angus and concentrate at the same time.

He turned her insides to mush whenever he looked at her. She could tell, even before turning around and seeing him, when he entered a room. Her entire being was so fine-tuned to Angus O'Donnell that she'd lain awake at night, listening for sounds from his home. Confessing that she loved him when she knew he so clearly didn't love her back would be devastating.

'We could have been so good together,' she murmured, and buried her head in her hands. The phone on her desk rang, making her jump, and she quickly snatched up the receiver.

'Hey, sis.' Leesa's voice came down the line. 'Free for dinner this Saturday? It's my turn to play hostess.'

Janet hesitated for a moment, wondering whether this was just the two of them or if the O'Donnell brothers would be there as well. 'You're not going to cook, are you?' Janet's attempt at humour fell flat as her sister detected the strain in her voice.

'What's wrong?'

'Nothing, really.' Janet tried to cover. 'I'm trying to write the advertisement for a permanent partner for the practice.'

'Aha,' Leesa replied, and Janet was sure her sister was nodding. 'So that's why you're not sounding your usual cheerful self. If it makes you feel any better, I was going to invite Angus and Hamish, but if you'd prefer to go out for a girls' night then I'm all for it. I rarely get a Saturday night off and, having two so close together, it's gone to my head.'

'Wouldn't you rather have an excuse to be with Hamish? This would be a perfect cover.'

'It's fine.'

'OK. It's a date, and after my talk at the university this Friday night I'll be determined to feel like celebrating.'

'Oh, that's this week? So how are your preparations going? Getting nervous?'

'A little nervous. I've photocopied handouts and had overhead projector transparencies made, so at the moment everything's done.'

'Good. Uh-oh, I'm being paged. I'll call you on Friday to see how it went.'

The sisters rang off and Janet looked at the recruitment advertisement before her. 'This is the right thing to do,' she told herself.

By the end of the day she'd faxed the information to several newspapers, ensuring the widest circulation possible. So why did she feel so depressed?

CHAPTER SEVEN

FRIDAY finally arrived, bringing with it a bunch of nerves. They showed up first thing in the morning and refused to leave, staying with Janet all day long. It wasn't that she was unprepared or worried about public speaking—it was just a fact. Every time she had to present a paper or be the centre of attention Janet became nervous.

After lunch, Karen buzzed through to her consulting room, saying that Mrs Stewart had cancelled but she'd a new patient who'd just come in to make an appointment.

'I'll be right out.' Janet stood and went out to the waiting room.

'Oh, Dr Stevenson.' A woman came up to her. 'Thank you for seeing my son so promptly. He's gone and hurt himself at school.'

'If you've filled in all the forms, why don't you come on through?' Janet suggested, showing mother and son the way. The boy was leaning heavily on his mother, using her as a crutch. 'Would you prefer a wheelchair?' she asked.

'No, thanks. I can manage,' he said with a grin.

She collected the paperwork from Karen and followed the patients into her consulting room.

'Now…' She quickly scanned the patient form for a name. 'Jamie. What have you done to your leg?'

'I hurt it, playing soccer on the oval at lunchtime.'

'He's always playing some type of sport,' his mother said matter-of-factly.

'The weather was great today, even if the grass was still a bit wet and slippery. We had a great time. Well, until I hurt my leg,' he finished.

'Right.' Janet made some notes. 'Were you kicking the ball? Running? Sliding? What position were you in when the pain first started?'

'I had possession of the ball…' His eyes radiated excitement. 'I dodged all the other boys and made it to the goal. I kicked and when I landed on my leg the pain just shot right up. The best thing,' he added, 'was that I scored a goal.'

'Well done,' Janet responded. 'So, was the pain anywhere specific? In your thigh? Your shin?'

'In the top of my thigh and like all around my knee.'

Janet made a few more notes. 'All right. Come and sit up here on the examination couch. Mrs Corn, you might want to help him up and, Jamie, I'll need you to take your trousers off. That way I can get a good look at your leg.'

Janet read over the patient's details while she waited for them to get ready. Jamie was the oldest of three boys and his mother's name was Kate. He'd never broken any bones or had any operations such as a tonsillectomy or appendectomy.

'Ready,' his mother announced, and Janet turned to face them.

His right leg was very red. 'The first thing I need to do is check your muscles. Lie down and put your legs out straight for me.' She helped him manoeuvre himself around. 'Now, keeping your leg straight, I want you to lift your good leg up off the couch.'

Jamie did as she asked without a problem.

'Good. Let's try the right leg.'

'I can't,' Jamie said after a moment. 'I can hardly lift it.'

'That's all right,' Janet said quickly. 'Don't do yourself a further injury by trying too hard.' Janet peered at his knee and took a good look at the swelling just beneath the kneecap. She touched the kneecap gently and determined that it wasn't the problem.

'Sit up for me now, Jamie, and dangle your legs over the side of the couch.' She helped him up, then bent to take a closer look. 'You're going to have a great-looking bruise there in a few days. All right, you can get dressed now.'

'Am I going to be all right?' Jamie asked, his voice a little concerned.

'You'll be fine,' Janet smiled. 'I'd like you to have an X-ray to confirm the diagnosis, which I believe to be Osgood-Schlatter disease.'

'Good what?' Jamie asked as his mother helped him to dress again.

'Osgood-Schlatter disease. It's caused by repetitive tension in the tibia…' she pointed to the upper section of his shin bone, near the kneecap '…and the quadriceps muscle, which is the muscle at the front of your thigh. When we run, we bend and straighten our knees. When you kicked your goal, your knee was straightened against resistance— in this case, the ball. This causes softening to occur where the bone juts out because inside that area is where the tendon is inserted. This is what causes the pain.

'The condition is treated by resting the knee and putting ice packs on it. No running and certainly no playing soccer for quite some time.'

Jamie looked glum at her words.

'I want you to RICE it.'

'To what?' Jamie's expression changed to one of disbelief. 'I have to put rice on it?'

'No.' Janet smiled. 'RICE stands for rest, ice packs, compression bandages to help keep the knee as still as possible—but don't make them too tight—and E for elevation. Make sure that when you rest you have it propped up on one or two pillows.'

Janet wrote out an X-ray request form and handed it to

Jamie's mother. 'Just paracetamol for the pain. If you wouldn't mind bringing the X-rays back after you've had them done, I can confirm the diagnosis. Just give them to Karen at Reception and she'll pass them on to me.'

'So I don't need to bring him back to see you again?'

'Only if you have any further problems. If Jamie gives it complete rest, and I mean complete—try not to even walk on it for a day or two—then it should settle down.' She looked at Jamie. 'If you still have a lot of pain in another few days, we'll have to put a plaster cast on it to keep it immobilised.'

'Cool,' Jamie responded.

'*Only,*' Janet stressed, 'if you're not in any more pain.'

'Thank you, Dr Stevenson,' Mrs Corn said as she stood and helped her son to balance on his foot. 'Will the X-ray people be able to fit us in today?'

'They should be able to. Ask Karen to ring up for you now and make an appointment.'

'Thanks a lot,' Mrs Corn reiterated again. 'Come on, Jamie.' She heaved his arm across her shoulders and supported the teenager as they hobbled out.

As the day continued, so Janet's nerves became worse. She read over her papers again and again while practising her deep-breathing exercises. When the last patient had gone, she hurried home to have something to eat—something light. She checked the letter-box and wasn't surprised to find it full of junk mail.

Dumping her bag, coat and mail on the table, she made a sandwich and a cup of tea, before sitting down to eat it. As she flicked through the junk mail she realised there was another envelope stuck between two catalogues. She pulled it out.

It had no stamp, indicating it had been hand-delivered. She slit the envelope and extracted a card. Filled with curiosity, she barely glanced at the flowers painted on the front and opened it to discover it was from Angus.

'"Just wanted to wish you all the best for tonight. You'll be fantastic!"' she read out loud. She closed the card and looked at the flowers. 'Freesias.' Janet smiled and shook her head. 'If only you'd agree to stay, Angus,' she said wistfully. 'We could have such a wonderful life together.'

Now wasn't the time to think about her relationship with Angus. Janet finished her sandwich and pulled her coat on while she drained her teacup. 'Big breath, Janet,' she instructed herself. 'Now, relax and knock their socks off.'

An hour later, the lecture hall was two thirds full and Janet's nerves had basically disappeared. She was prepared and relaxed. Everything *would* be fantastic, just as Angus had predicted.

Feeling a pang of desolation, Janet realised she wanted him here. To share this with him, to feel his support, would have been like the icing on the cake.

Time was ticking on and soon her colleague was introducing her. She received a small round of applause as she stepped up to the podium. Her opening went well, and just before she indicated for the lights to be dimmed to display her overhead transparencies she spotted a familiar face.

Angus. He *had* come. Albeit against her wishes, but he'd still come. Janet smiled at him and received a dazzling smile back before the lights went out.

Everything ran smoothly and the question time afterwards was over before she knew it. As people began to mill out, a few came up and offered their thanks for the lecture, making Janet feel ten feet tall. She was conscious of Angus slowly making his way over, not wanting to disturb those students who wanted a quiet word with her.

'You were fantastic,' he said when the last student had left. 'I knew you would be. You speak so passionately on the subject, no one dares doubt you.'

'They'd better not.' Janet continued to pack her things away, rearranging her overhead transparencies in order. 'Do you think they'll take me on as a permanent lecturer? I mean, speaking specifically on this topic?'

'If everything else—red tape, such as budget and scheduling and so on—is organised, I can't see why not. It's certainly not your presentation or the materials you presented that would make them decline.'

'Thank you, Angus.'

'You're not mad at me for coming?'

'No.' Janet closed her briefcase. 'I was glad to see a familiar face.'

'Shall we go? I'll walk you to your car.' Angus helped her on with her coat, before leading the way to the bank of lifts. 'Quite a good turnout,' he commented as they rode down to the ground floor.

'A very good turnout. I hadn't anticipated that many people. Loren, my friend who introduced me, had to make more copies of my handout as the university hadn't made enough.'

'That should work well in your favour.'

'I hope so.' The lift reached the ground. 'I'm parked in the west car park.'

'I know. I parked next to you.' They walked through the university grounds, which were lit up like a Christmas tree. 'I wanted to make sure you made it to your car safely,' he offered by way of explanation.

'There have been a few reported incidents lately of attacks on campus,' Janet commented.

'Hamish told me.'

Janet stopped walking. 'Is that why you came? Because Hamish told you about those attacks and you wanted to make sure I made it to my car OK?'

'No, and stop jumping to conclusions.' He took her free hand in his and tugged her along. Janet's body warmed at his touch. 'It's too cold to stand still and argue, Janet.' He waited until they were walking again before he said, 'I came to support you and to listen to what you had to say. I know you can look after yourself, although it goes without saying that being out at this time of night—for any woman—generally isn't safe these days. Unfortunately, it's the society we live in.'

No sooner were the words out of his mouth than they heard a high-pitched scream. Angus stopped walking and let go of Janet's hand. He listened. The scream came again along with calls of, 'Stop it!'

'Come on,' he urged, and ran in the direction of the screams. They left the well-lit area and headed into the darkness of the park grounds that surrounded the university. 'Leave her alone,' Angus called loudly. They heard a male voice swear before multiple footsteps of people running pounded quickly away.

'Where's that full moon when you need it?' Angus mumbled, but by now their eyes had become accustomed to the darkness and they soon found the girl. She was lying curled into the foetal position, her soft crying wrenching at Janet's heart.

'It's all right. Everything's all right,' Angus soothed as he bent down beside her. 'Can you move at all?' he asked softly as Janet crouched down on the other side of the girl.

'We're doctors,' she told the girl. 'It's going to be all right. He's gone.'

'He'll come back,' the girl protested.

'All the more reason to get you out of here,' Angus said. He continued running his hands over her body. 'Feels like a break in your arm. Can you move at all?'

The girl tried to sit up but a scream of pain was pulled from her lungs. 'The baby,' she whimpered. 'The baby.'

'How far are you?' Janet reached her hand around to the girl's stomach and felt the swell of the unborn child.

'Twenty-four weeks. He doesn't want me to have it,' she cried.

'Left radius or ulna feels broken. I'll carry her,' Angus said. 'Help me lift her, Janet, and we'll take her to my car. She needs to be checked out immediately.'

Together they settled the girl in Angus's arms before Janet collected her briefcase. They walked quickly and carefully over the uneven ground back to the lit area of the campus. Once there, Angus continued on to the car park while Janet gave the girl as good a visual inspection as she could. She was wearing slip-on shoes, maternity jeans and a T-shirt. Admittedly, the spiky, green hair came as a surprise, but looks were immaterial.

'Get the keys out of my trouser pocket, Janet, and open the door. I'll put her on the back seat. You ride with her. We can come back for your car later.'

Not wanting to think about the sexual implications of thrusting her hand into Angus's trousers, Janet called on the professional deep within her and did as he'd asked. Soon the girl was settled, her head resting on Janet's lap.

Angus made sure they were comfortable, before whispering in Janet's ear, 'Her jeans are wet. I think her membrane's ruptured.'

Janet nodded as he closed the door and started the engine. The girl's crying had stopped. Her eyes remained closed and her breathing began to return to normal. Janet looked at the bruises on her face and arms. She could only guess what injuries and bruising lay beneath the jeans.

She heard Angus phone the hospital as he drove fast but safely towards it. He obviously didn't care, after going through a few red lights, that a police-car siren could be heard behind them.

'What's going on?' the girl asked quietly.

'We're taking you to the hospital,' Janet replied.

'The baby?'

'We need to check it out. To make sure everything is still all right.'

'What about that police siren?'

'Ignore it. Your chauffeur here…' she pointed to the front seat '…can't distinguish his colours correctly. He's gone through a few red lights.'

'Will they get mad at him?'

'No. It's an emergency. The police are usually quite lenient in these circumstances. I'm Janet and the crazy driver is Angus. What's your name?'

'Stacey. I feel so…' Whatever Stacey had been about to say was cut short by a terrible groan that was wrenched from her.

Janet placed a hand on Stacey's abdomen. 'She's having contractions, Angus. How much further?'

'Not far.'

'Relax, Stacey. Breathe.'

'What's wrong?' Stacey started crying again when the contraction had passed.

'You've just had a contraction. We're almost at the hospital.'

'It hurts. It *really* hurts.'

'I know.'

Angus kept driving and when they reached the hospital grounds he drove directly to Emergency, the police car in hot pursuit.

As they pulled up, personnel seemed to be everywhere. Stacey was lifted from the car with the utmost care while Angus spoke with the policemen. Janet left him to it and followed the barouche inside.

'Janet,' Stacey called. 'Don't leave me.' Her eyes were wild with uncertainty as they wheeled her into an examination cubicle.

Janet hastened her step. 'I'm here,' she reassured Stacey as a white-coated doctor walked into the room.

'I'm Dr Quinlan. What seems to be the problem?' The man who spoke looked about eighteen years old. His blond hair was short and messy while his hazel eyes displayed tiredness and fatigue. He did, however, manage a small, polite smile.

'This is Stacey…?' Janet stopped, realising she didn't know Stacey's surname.

'Wells,' Stacey supplied.

'Stacey Wells. Twenty-four weeks and had her first contraction…' she consulted her watch '…two minutes ago. Membrane has ruptured. Assault on university grounds, possible fracture to left arm.'

'And you are?' Dr Quinlan raised his eyebrows at Janet's spiel.

'Dr Janet Stevenson.'

'Any relation to our ortho registrar?' he asked as he wrote notes about Stacey's condition.

'She's my sister. If you wouldn't mind paging her to take a look at Stacey's arm, I'd appreciate it.'

Dr Quinlan nodded and made a few more notes, before handing the chart to the nurse behind him. 'Who have you been seeing for your antenatal check-ups?' he asked.

Stacey raised her eyes to meet Janet's. She was like a frightened child in very unfamiliar territory. 'It's all right.' Janet squeezed her hand, hoping to reassure her.

'I've just been down to the clinic near the university.'

'Also page an Obs and Gyn registrar, stat,' Dr Quinlan ordered the nurse, who turned and left. Moments later another nurse entered and Dr Quinlan proceeded. 'Stacey, I need to examine you. Tell me where it hurts the most.'

'My arm, chest, back—everywhere.' She closed her eyes.

'OK.' Dr Quinlan checked her pupils and pronounced them fine. The nurse took her temperature and blood pressure, announcing they were slightly raised. She spoke softly to Dr Quinlan who came over and picked up Stacey's right arm.

'You have puncture scars here, although they look old. Are you using anything at the moment?'

'No. I've been clean since I discovered I was pregnant. I don't want to hurt this baby.'

'Good.' Dr Quinlan nodded. 'We need to take your jeans off to assess the baby,' he informed her as a foetal heart monitor was wheeled into the room. 'This…' he indicated the machine '…lets us count the baby's heartbeats so we can see how it's doing. Was the baby punched in the assault?'

'I…I'm not sure.' Her voice broke. 'I was trying to shield it as best I could but I can't remem—' She stopped and began to cry softly.

'Shh,' Janet soothed. 'Everything's going to be all right. Let me help take your jeans off and we'll have a listen to the baby's heartbeat.'

'Don't leave me, Janet.'

'I'm not going anywhere.'

They managed to get Stacey into a hospital gown with little trouble, and the foetal heart monitor was placed on her abdomen. Janet looked at the bruises that were starting to form on Stacey's legs. Whoever had done this to her had done a good job.

The beats could be heard loud and clear, but as they listened Janet's eyes met Dr Quinlan's. There were too many beats. The baby was going into stress.

'I need an ETA on that Obs and Gyn registrar,' Dr Quinlan told the nurse, who hurried away.

Stacey groaned and Janet placed her hand on her abdomen.

'Here comes another contraction,' she told Stacey, before looking at her watch. 'Roughly ten minutes since the last one. I want you to concentrate on your breathing, Stacey.

I'll rub your back, which will hopefully ease some of the pain.'

The contraction came and went, leaving a very exhausted Stacey lying on the bed. 'I don't want this,' she whispered. 'The baby's not ready yet.'

'I know,' Janet soothed. 'The fact is, you're in labour. There's nothing we can do and there's no way we can stop it.'

'What about drugs?' Stacey asked. 'Can I have something to stop the pain?'

'We'll ask the obstetric registrar.'

'Mind if I join the show?' Angus spoke softly, and walked into the room.

'It's a three-ringed circus in here,' Dr Quinlan muttered. 'Who are you?'

'He saved me.' It was Stacey who spoke and she looked adoringly up at Angus. Janet smiled and raised her eyebrows when his gaze met hers.

'I'm Dr O'Donnell,' he informed Dr Quinlan.

'Oh, great. One guess who you're related to,' the admitting registrar mumbled.

'Thank you,' Stacey said a little shyly, still looking at Angus. 'You saved my life.'

Angus didn't say anything but nodded and smiled. 'You'll be fine now.'

'Did that policeman book you?'

'No, but he does want a word with you about the assault. I've told him it can wait until later.'

Stacey closed her eyes. 'Thanks.' Her voice was soft and Janet could tell she was beginning to think about what had happened.

'Put it out of your mind for now, Stacey. You can deal with it later. Right now you need to focus on your baby.'

'Never was a truer word said,' a female voice said from

the doorway of the cubicle. 'Obstetric registrar at your service.' She crossed to Stacey's side. 'I'm Dr Pinkerton.'

'It's getting more than crowded in here,' Angus said.

'Here, here,' agreed Dr Quinlan.

'I'm going,' Angus told him, before turning to Stacey. 'You're in good hands.' He smiled his dazzling smile at the girl then met Janet's eyes. 'I'll go and collect your car.'

'OK. The keys are in my—'

'I've rummaged through your purse and found them,' he cut her off before he walked out.

Janet was slightly miffed at his overbearing attitude but, then again, that seemed to be how the O'Donnells did things. There was nothing she could do about it now and he knew that. She'd just have to let this one slide as Stacey was starting to grip her hand again.

Dr Augustine Pinkerton, or Pink, as she was known to her friends and colleagues, was quite a petite woman with short brown hair and large brown eyes. Janet had met her once before at a hospital party Leesa had dragged her to.

'Hi, Janet. Stacey, I need to check the baby and to see how far you're dilated.' Pink scrubbed at the sink by the bed and put a pair of gloves on. 'Listen to Janet. She'll tell you how to relax and breathe.'

Pink examined Stacey and listened to the baby's heartbeat again, before requesting the ultrasound monitor be brought in. She also asked, in a much quieter voice, for the nurse to prepare a theatre for a Caesarean section.

'Stacey,' Pink said as she removed her gloves and pulled up a chair near Stacey's head. 'I'm going to perform an ultrasound to check the baby, but as far as I can tell it's breech. That means that the head isn't engaged and the feet would come out first.'

'Is…it…?' She stopped and bit her lip. 'Is it…?' She couldn't go on.

'Is it going to live?' Janet asked the question for her and Stacey nodded.

'I want to perform a Caesarean section to take the baby out. The heartbeat is slightly higher than normal, which means the baby isn't coping well with the situation. For you to try and push the baby out would only stress the poor little mite even more.'

Pink went on to explain the operation to her and Janet helped Stacey sign the permission forms. Leesa had arrived in the midst of things but waited patiently outside for Pink to finish. As Stacey's health was stable, the baby was everyone's first concern.

'Can I have some drugs? My arm is still really sore.'

'Sure. I'll arrange for some pain relief.'

While they waited for the ultrasound monitor to arrive, Leesa came and introduced herself to Stacey.

'I see my big sister's been keeping you in line,' Leesa joked as she gently examined Stacey's arm. 'It's definitely broken. For now I'll put it in a splint. Once the baby's been delivered, I'll order an X-ray and fix it properly for you.'

'I noticed a bruise forming on her chest when we got her changed, Leesa. Would you mind checking her ribs as well?'

'Sure.' Leesa did as she was asked and pronounced the left T3 and T4 ribs fractured. 'Again I'll need an X-ray to confirm but not until the baby's safe and sound.'

'It will make breast-feeding harder and a lot more uncomfortable,' Janet said quietly. 'You're going to need some support, Stacey. Is there anyone I can call? Your parents?'

'My parents don't even know I'm pregnant and would freak if they found out.'

Leesa met Janet's glance over their patient's head. 'Do they live in Newcastle?' Leesa asked.

'Sydney. They don't want anything to do with me and

that's just fine.' Stacey's words were final. Pink came back in with the ultrasound monitor and soon her suspicions were confirmed.

'The baby isn't coping too well.' At her words Stacey had another contraction and Pink was able to monitor the baby throughout. 'I've arranged to take you to Theatre and the anaesthetist will be here soon.' When he arrived Pink introduced him. He quickly explained the procedure and began inserting the butterfly drip into Stacey's spine, ready for the epidural block. While he did this, Pink and Leesa conferred outside before Leesa quickly came back in to splint Stacey's arm and say goodbye.

'Everything will be fine,' she said when the arm was secure. 'I'll see you later, Stacey.'

'She's nice, your sister.' Stacey's words were said through clenched teeth as she tried to remain as still as she could.

'That she is,' Janet responded. 'He's nearly finished— just a few more minutes.'

'Aren't they going to gas me or something?'

'No. The epidural block numbs you from the waist down,' the anaesthetist explained again.

'I'll be awake?' Stacey asked, her eyes as wide as saucers, the reality of her situation beginning to hit home.

'Yes. It's better for your health,' Janet answered.

'You'll be there, won't you, Janet?' Stacey asked, seeking reassurance once more.

'I wouldn't miss it for the world.'

When the block was done, Stacey started to relax. The next contraction she didn't feel. Soon everything was organised and they were ready to move her. Angus walked over to the barouche.

'I'm back. You just lie there and take it easy, Stacey. Let the doctors do all the work. You've been through enough for one evening.'

'Will you wait?' she asked softly, and Angus smiled.

'Yes. I'm going to have a cup of coffee with Leesa. I can't wait to meet this baby of yours.'

He left then, but not before giving Janet a wink. She walked alongside the barouche, and when they arrived in Theatre she left Stacey only to change into theatre clothes.

While they waited for Pink to get a few more things organised, Stacey was introduced to the paediatrician, Dr Richard Mooree, and the rest of the theatre staff.

'Chances are,' Dr Mooree explained, 'that the baby will require specialist care.'

'Can you do that?'

'Probably not. At this stage of development the baby's lungs and kidneys aren't completely mature and therefore we'll need to transfer him or her to Sydney where they can provide that specialist care.'

'You'll need to be separated from your baby but only for a little while,' Janet continued. 'Once Leesa and Pink have given you the all-clear, you, too, can be transferred to Sydney to be near your baby.' Janet hesitated for only a split second before asking, 'Are you sure I can't contact your parents? You're going to need their support.'

Stacey didn't answer. Janet took that as a good sign. The poor girl had so much to think about. So much had happened in the past two hours that her world had flipped on its axis. She didn't want to talk about the assault, which was fair enough, but Janet was sure that she knew exactly who had attacked her.

'All set?' Pink asked over the green theatre drape that obscured Stacey's vision of the procedure.

'Yup,' Stacey said nervously, and Janet patted her hand.

'Try to relax. I know it's hard, but just think of the baby.' Janet watched over the drape as Pink made her incision, and within seconds she had the baby out.

Stacey could hear the faint cry of her child and tears flowed down her cheeks. 'What is it? Tell me.'

Pink held the baby up high. 'You have a girl. At a quarter past midnight. Congratulations, Mum.'

'Mum!' Stacey said the word with wonderment, and in that split second Janet saw the girl mature into a woman.

The baby was handed over to Dr Mooree who quickly performed the necessary tests.

'What are you going to call her?' Janet asked as Pink extracted the placenta and began to tidy things up.

'I...I hadn't... I wasn't...' Stacey couldn't finish her sentence. Janet watched the emotions cross her face and guessed what the new mother couldn't say.

'Were you going to put her up for adoption?'

Stacey nodded. 'It was...Mick's idea. He never wanted the baby in the first place.' The tears started to slowly trickle down Stacey's cheeks as her self-imposed wall started to crumble. 'He said it was an accident and I should get rid of it. When I refused he started threatening me.'

She gazed unseeingly up at Janet. 'It was only when he was high that he would say awful things to me, but lately he seems to have been high all the time.'

'Was he the one who attacked you?'

Stacey nodded. 'He and his friend, Rob. They'd just injected some really good stuff and wanted to get something to eat. I don't think they planned it, but as we were walking across the campus grounds Mick started saying how ugly I was with my fat stomach and then Rob joined in. They pushed me between them before I stumbled and fell over. That's when they...they...'

'Shh,' Janet soothed, and squeezed Stacey's hand for reassurance. She wiped the tears from the girl's face and waited for the crying to subside.

When things were quiet again Janet said, 'Think about a name. There's no harm in you choosing a name.'

The baby was placed in a humidicrib and quickly wheeled over for Stacey to see.

'She's having trouble breathing, Stacey,' Dr Mooree told her. 'I need to get her stabilised before she's transferred to Sydney.'

Stacey only nodded and blew her baby a kiss. As the baby was wheeled out, a few more tears slipped out and slid down the girl's cheeks. Janet wiped them away.

'Things will work out fine. You'll see.'

Stacey was wheeled to a maternity ward where Janet advised her to get some rest. 'You've been through quite an ordeal and Leesa will want to look at your ribs and arm soon. Are you hungry at all?'

'No,' Stacey said as she was settled in a private room. 'I thought I'd go into a ward.'

'Leesa pulled a few strings,' Janet explained with a smile. She picked up a small bag that was on the locker beside the bed. 'This is for you, from the volunteers who work here at the hospital. It has everything you might need until we can organise for your own things to be brought in.' Janet opened the little bag. 'Pens, paper and stamped envelopes—just in case you feel like writing to someone. Then the essentials such as tissues, toothpaste, toothbrush, comb, washer, soap, razors, powder and cotton buds.'

'Who did you say this is from?'

'The hospital volunteers.'

'My mother used to work as a hospital volunteer,' Stacey said as Janet handed her the bag.

The poor girl seemed so confused at the moment that Janet thought it best to give her a bit of space. 'You try and relax for a while. I'll ask one of the nurses to come and give you a hand if you feel like freshening up. I'm just going to get changed—but I'll be back soon.'

'Check on the baby for me?'

'I'll do that first,' Janet told her, and before she'd walked out of the room Stacey's eyes were closed.

The neonatal unit was located one level up from the maternity ward. Here the whole cast of today's events was gathered—Angus and Leesa, Pink and Richard Mooree.

'What's the prognosis?' Janet asked after she'd washed and put a gown over her theatre clothes. They all turned to look at her.

'Touch and go at the moment.' It was Richard who spoke. 'Her lungs and kidneys are fighting hard to keep her alive and, as you can see, she's jaundiced.'

'Poor little thing,' Janet cooed.

'How's Stacey?' Angus asked.

'Exhausted. Thanks for organising the private room, Leesa. She should be able to get some sleep.'

'Has she said anything about the attack?' Angus continued.

Janet nodded. 'In Theatre.'

'We all heard it,' Pink put in.

'She said that her *boyfriend*…' Janet said the word as though it were contaminated. 'Mick, no surname given, didn't want the baby and was pressuring her to put it up for adoption after she'd refused to have an abortion.'

'What about her parents?' Leesa asked. 'Angus said they live in Sydney.'

'I'm hoping Stacey will soon agree to me contacting them. She's beginning to realise the decisions she's facing, and what she can control. She can either contact her parents and keep the baby or put her up for adoption and go back to the scum-of-the-earth boyfriend, which I hope she realises is a bad idea. Either way, tonight's events have drastically changed her life.'

'The fact that she's been off drugs since she discovered she was pregnant,' Pink added, 'shows great courage and stamina. If she makes the right choices now, she'll be OK.'

'When is the baby scheduled to leave?' Janet asked Richard.

'Two hours.'

'Can Stacey see the baby before then?'

'Of course.' Richard nodded.

'Bring her up in a wheelchair on the way to Radiology,' Leesa suggested. 'I've filled in the X-ray request forms so everything is ready to go.'

'Will she require further surgery?' Angus asked Leesa.

'The break seemed clean when I examined her but I won't know for sure until I see the films. For Stacey's sake, I hope it's simply a plaster cast and nothing else.'

'I'd better get changed and see how she's doing,' Janet told the group.

'I'll come with you,' Angus offered, and the two of them left the neonatal unit to walk back to Theatres.

'Thanks for hanging around,' Janet said.

'Don't mention it. It's been good to catch up with Leesa, one on one. She's a very thought-provoking woman.'

Janet's eyes widened in alarm. 'What's she been saying?' It was difficult to keep her voice neutral as she asked the question but thankfully Angus didn't pick up on her sudden agitation.

'Nothing much. We talked about your lecture this evening and she started asking me about my different experiences over the years. Did you know the university offers visiting lecturer positions to doctors who have worked overseas for more than two years?'

'No.' Janet sounded as surprised as he was.

'Leesa told me it's a twelve-month position part time, where I could basically tell of my travels and techniques. It's to both medical students and interns—to give them an idea of medical trends and practices in foreign countries.'

'Interesting,' Janet said slowly as they reached the theatre block. 'I'll just go and change. Do you want me to meet you somewhere?'

'No. I'll wait.' Angus gave her a distracted smile, his thoughts clearly elsewhere.

Janet went into the female change rooms, walking slowly to the visitors' locker where her clothes were neatly hanging. Working on autopilot, she quickly changed. Her thoughts and emotions were jumbled with the news Angus had just imparted.

'Could he actually be thinking of staying?' She smiled at her reflection. To have Angus for another twelve months would be fantastic. He could work in the practice and lecture at the university, bringing diversity to his job.

Her eyes were wide with excitement as she ran her fingers through her hair. If he stayed, it would change everything.

They both knew that.

CHAPTER EIGHT

JANET and Angus stayed at the hospital until the baby had been stabilised and was on her way to Sydney, while Stacey slept soundly.

When they arrived back home, it was almost four o'clock on Saturday morning. Both of them were completely exhausted so when Angus said he'd come in and make them both a relaxing cup of tea, Janet didn't have the strength to argue.

'I'm so overtired that a cup of tea sounds nice,' she said when he told her to sit down in the lounge room and relax.

He switched the kettle on to boil and joined her. 'What a night!'

'You can say that again.'

'What a night!' They both smiled at each other. 'You know...' He moved a little closer. 'You're very good glue.'

'I beg your pardon?' Janet allowed him to draw her closer. She needed to feel his arms around her—just one more time.

'Glue. You're good at holding people together.'

'Thank you—I think.'

'In your daily practice, you're constantly patching people up and helping them on the road to recovery, regardless of what's wrong with them. Tonight, you were there for Stacey—mentally—helping her keep it together.' He shrugged. 'You're good glue.'

'Now all I want to know is how this glue is going to help persuade her to contact her parents, press charges against the creep who did this to her and retain custody of her baby.'

'There's only one way you *can* achieve all that.' Angus gave her his familiar smile. 'You need some ''super'' glue.'

Janet laughed. 'And I suppose that's you?'

'Who else would it be? We should stick together.' The corny line lost its impact when their gazes met and held, the jovial moment disappearing into thin air as Angus moved closer. He reached out a hand and pulled the band from her hair, fascinated at the way its strawberry-gold highlights cascaded down to her shoulders.

'I love the way your eyes sparkle when you laugh.' He gently pushed his fingers through her hair, before cradling the back of her head and drawing her closer to him.

Angus brought his mouth to hers, the first fleeting touch sending warmth coursing through her entire body. She felt as though an eternity had passed since he'd last kissed her when, in reality, it had only been a few short weeks.

His mouth opened again and he slowly ran the tip of his tongue around her lips. Janet could feel her breathing increase, her heartbeat hammering against her ribs at the provocative gesture. He knew how to excite her with such a simple yet sensual kiss.

'I've missed you, Janet.' His voice was thick with desire.

'I know.' The whistle of the kettle stopped her from saying more as Angus reluctantly pulled away and went into the kitchen.

He returned with a tray of cups and saucers, milk and a pot of tea. 'Shall I pour?' he asked as he sat back down next to her.

Janet nodded, not trusting her voice. The man had her so confused she wasn't sure which way was up. Just when she thought she could resist him, he made it impossible for her to do so.

'We take our tea the same way,' he murmured as he handed her a cup. 'A drop of milk and no sugar. I guess we're sweet enough.'

She took a much-needed sip, before saying, 'I guess we are.'

'Tea tastes so much better when it's drunk from bone china cups, don't you think?'

Janet frowned. 'Are you trying to make…small talk, Angus?'

'As a matter of fact, I am. It's what civilised English people do when they're at a loss. "Hard day at work? How about a nice cup of tea?" It solves all problems, eases all tensions and helps the drinker to obtain a new and unique perspective on the issues facing them—not to mention the marvellous anti-oxidants the brew so generously gives to our bodies.'

By the time he'd finished speaking, Janet was smiling once more. Any awkwardness previously between them had now vanished.

'How do you do it, Angus?'

'Do what?'

'Know just the right thing to say to relax me.'

'I'll let you in on a little secret.' He motioned for her to come closer, before whispering, 'I've known you for a long time.'

Janet pulled back and smiled at him again. 'Yes, I remember, but have you always been this observant?'

'Yes. You've just never noticed.' The teasing look was back in his eyes as he sipped his tea. 'Another cup?' he asked as Janet finished hers and placed her cup back on the tray.

'No. My mind is starting to wind down now. Perhaps we should both get some sleep. Stacey asked us to be back at the hospital nice and early. Besides that, I still have my regular house call to Cyril Montague to fit in somewhere.'

'I'd offer to do it for you but it's probably better for his sake if you go.' Angus stood and Janet followed suit. He placed an arm about her shoulders. 'Walk me to the door.'

He urged her a little and she went with him. The feel of his warm body so close to hers started to bring her body to life once more, so when they reached the door she quickly pulled away.

'Thanks for everything, Angus. Especially for being a familiar face in the crowd at my lecture.'

'It seems so long ago.'

'That it does.'

'At least today is Saturday and not a week-day, otherwise we'd have a whole clinic plus Stacey to deal with.'

'True.'

'If we plan on getting to the hospital around eight, that should at least give us a few hours to sleep.'

'We can catch up tonight.' Janet remembered about Leesa. 'Oh, no. I promised Leesa we'd go out.'

'Why didn't I know about it?' Angus demanded.

'Because you and your brother weren't invited. Can't Leesa and I spend some time together without the O'Donnell brothers?'

'I guess so.' He shook his head. 'Although you two are the closest thing I have to sisters, I doubt I'll ever understand the relationship you share.'

'Don't even try, my friend,' Janet smiled warmly. 'It's far too complex for you. Go home and sleep. I'll see you at the hospital.'

'You mean I can't come over for breakfast?'

'I'm not baking anything. Not this morning. If you want to come it will be toast and orange juice. Coffee if you're lucky.'

'Sounds good. See you then.' Like lightning, he planted a warm yet firm kiss on her lips, before slipping out the door.

Janet stood there for a moment after he left, her fingers raised to her mouth. 'I'm never going to survive,' she mur-

mured as she heard his own front door close. Bolting the
door and switching off the lights, Janet headed for bed.

'She'll be there for at least the next twelve weeks,' Janet
told Stacey later that morning. Poor Stacey. With her arm
in plaster, the bruises starting to make themselves known
and her sick, premature baby in Sydney—it was no wonder
she wasn't feeling too good.

'That long?'

'She needs to finish growing. She requires special con-
ditions, treatment and nursing, and she'll be getting the best
in Sydney,' Angus said as he sat on the chair by the bed.

'When can I go and be with her?'

'There are a few more things to clear up here first,' Janet
told her as she straightened the bed sheets and propped
Stacey up on another pillow. 'You have some hard decisions to make.'

'I need to talk to that cop, don't I?'

'That's the first thing you need to do before Pink will
sign your release papers.' Angus nodded.

Janet sat down on the bed and looked at Stacey. 'What
about the baby? Are you going to keep her?'

Tears welled up in Stacey's eyes and she nodded. 'Having her taken from me—to Sydney—has shown me how
much I need her. I'm going to keep her.'

'You'll need a lot of support and help. Have you thought
any more about contacting your parents?'

'I don't want to.' She hung her head, unable to meet
Janet's gaze. 'We had a really bad fight before I came to
Newcastle.'

'Did it have anything to do with this Mick person—who
got you pregnant and then assaulted you?' Angus kept his
voice calm as he asked the question, although his clenched
fist was a dead give-away that he was controlling his
temper.

'Yes. They said he was bad news.'

'Appears they were right.' Angus stood and walked to the window, his back to the two women. 'Are you going to press charges against him?'

'I...I don't know.'

'Stacey,' Janet said quickly as Angus spun on his heel to glare at the girl in bed. 'Think of everything that's happened since you've been with Mick. He tried to hook you on drugs, you became pregnant, he tried to pressure you into an abortion—and when that failed he was trying to persuade you to give up that beautiful little girl who you've already fallen in love with. Not only that, he attacked you. I'm sorry, but this doesn't sound like he cares for you at all.'

'It's only the drugs,' Stacey tried to reason. 'When he comes off them, things will get better.'

'Stacey.' Angus had himself under control. 'What makes you think he's going to come off the drugs?'

'He's signed up at one of the methadone clinics.'

'Whose idea was that?' Janet asked.

'Mine.' Stacey lifted her chin defiantly.

'And has he been at all?' Angus asked the question and both he and Janet witnessed the sadness in Stacey's eyes as she replied that he hadn't.

'You've said that Mick didn't want the baby. How is he going to treat her?'

'Once he sees her he'll fall in love with her, just like I did.'

'Stacey.' Angus crossed to her bedside. 'Babies affect women differently to men. I'm not saying that your little girl isn't gorgeous because she is, but you've had six months of her developing inside you. You've felt her move and kick—and Mick's attitude has been what? To have nothing to do with it. All he cares about is his drugs.'

'But—'

'Stacey, when I went back to get Janet's car last night, the policeman who followed us to the hospital, Officer Shirmin, came with me. I had a suspicion it was someone you knew so we asked around at your dormitory and eventually found Mick and his friend. Do you want to know where they were?'

From the look on Stacey's face she could guess, but she didn't reply to Angus's question.

'They were at a nearby pizza place. Satisfying their cravings for food—without a care in the world about you. It only took a few hard questions from Officer Shirmin before Mick confessed to assaulting you. He's still in custody.'

'But…' Stacey protested again, tears in her eyes once more.

'I know it's difficult to come to terms with,' Janet said with compassion, 'but it's the truth. He doesn't care about you—or the baby. It hurts.'

Stacey broke into a fresh round of tears and Janet quickly enveloped her in a hug. Angus resumed his seat by the bed and waited.

When things were quieter, Janet asked, 'Have you thought of a name for your daughter?'

'Daughter!' Stacey marvelled. 'It feels so strange to say the word.'

'You'll get used to it in time.'

'I feel as though all I've done in the past day is cry the entire time.' Stacey managed a watery smile.

'It's common. Your hormones are going haywire at the moment.' Janet and Angus waited for a response to the question.

Stacey looked away and straightened the sheets which didn't require straightening. 'I've come up with Madeline Jessica—Maddie for short,' she added with a shy smile.

'A lovely name for a lovely girl,' Angus said.

'Well, I just like the name Maddie, and Jessica—it's my mum's name.'

'I'm sure she'll be honoured.' Janet held her breath for a moment, before asking, 'So, is it all right for me to contact her now?'

Stacey reluctantly nodded. 'I *am* going to need help. I know that. Especially since Maddie—' she smiled when she said the name '—will be in hospital for quite a while.'

'Do *you* want to tell your mum about the baby?'

'No. You tell her everything. About Mick and...well about everything.'

Janet nodded.

'I-if that's OK with you, I mean.'

'It's fine, Stacey,' Janet reassured her. 'Do you have her contact details?'

Stacey rattled off a phone number and Janet quickly wrote it down. 'I'll go and do this now,' she said. Before Stacey changes her mind, she added silently.

Janet went into the ward sister's office and dialled the number. On the third ring it was answered by a woman announcing it was the 'Wells residence'.

'May I speak with Mrs Jessica Wells?' Janet asked.

'Whom shall I say is calling?' the voice asked.

Janet wasn't sure whether it was someone joking around or real, so she decided to play it by the book. 'My name is Dr Janet Stevenson.'

'No fundraisers, please. Mrs Wells is on enough committees, thank you, Doctor.'

'It's about Stacey,' Janet said quickly as the other woman appeared ready to disconnect the call. There was silence on the other end for a moment.

'I beg your pardon? Did you say Stacey?'

She had the woman's interest now. 'Yes. Is it possible to speak with Mrs Wells?'

'Stacey's all right, isn't she?' There was alarm in the voice now and Janet quickly reassured the other woman.

'She's in hospital but she's fine. Is Mrs Wells available, please?' How many more times did she have to ask?

'Yes, Dr Stevenson. I'll get her right away.'

'Thank you,' Janet replied with relief.

There was a brief pause before another female voice, filled with urgency, said, 'I'm Jessica Wells. Is Stacey really all right?'

'Mrs Wells, she's doing nicely.'

'What's happened? Tell me what's happened.'

Janet told Stacey's mother the events of the past twenty-four hours. When she was finished there was a stunned silence on the other end of the line.

'I...I have a gr-granddaughter?'

'Yes. Her name is Madeline Jessica.'

'Oh!'

Janet could hear sniffs and sobs coming from the other end of the line.

'You must understand, Dr Stevenson, that when Stacey left we felt we had to be firm and stand our ground, but I knew something bad would happen. I knew we should have gone after her but she's so stubborn—just like her father. She's really all right?'

'She's recovering well but it will take about six to eight weeks for her broken arm and ribs to heal.'

'And my granddaughter? Madeline Jessica? She's here? In Sydney?'

'Yes. She should be at the children's hospital by now.'

'Oh, we *must* go and see her. Our little Madeline Jessica.'

'Of course. Mrs Wells, if you don't mind, there are a few more things I have to say. Namely, it was a big decision for Stacey to decide to keep the baby, rather than putting it up for adoption.'

'I can imagine. Especially with the pressure that… that…drug-addict boyfriend of hers was putting on her.'

'As I mentioned before, she's agreed to press charges and probably won't have anything to do with him again. What she does need, Mrs Wells, is your help, your support and your love. What she *doesn't* need is for you to take over. This is *her* baby.'

'But she's only a child herself!'

'She's twenty years old, Mrs Wells. My mother was only twenty when she had me,' Janet added, hoping to change the other woman's perception about her daughter. If Mrs Wells could see Stacey as a woman, not a little girl, it would help the situation dramatically.

'Yes,' Mrs Wells replied. 'I had just turned twenty when I had Stacey but I guess, being married, I felt so much older. How soon we forget.'

'Stacey has matured dramatically in the past day, considering the events she's been through. Motherhood can do that to a person.'

'I understand you perfectly, Doctor, and shall speak to my husband. They're the ones that clash so badly but it's only because they're so much alike. We'll do everything we can to support Stacey but at the same time encourage her in her responsibilities as a mother.'

'Thank you,' Janet replied. 'You have my name and contact phone numbers if you need to talk again. Will you or your husband be coming to Newcastle to see Stacey?'

'I'll be there once I've seen my granddaughter. Gloria, our housekeeper, is packing a bag for me now. Will you be there when I arrive, Dr Stevenson? I'd like to thank you in person for everything you've done for our daughter.'

'Seeing Stacey happy is enough thanks, Mrs Wells, but, yes, I'll be here.'

'What about that other doctor? The one who saved her life.'

'Dr O'Donnell. Yes, he'll be here also.'

'Good. I'll see you soon.'

Janet ended the call with a satisfied smile. She could feel Stacey's nervousness when she returned.

'So? What did they say?'

'I spoke with your mother and she'll be here in a few hours' time. First, though, she's going to stop by to see Maddie. I've called the children's hospital and they're expecting her visit.'

'Was she angry?'

'No, come to think of it, she wasn't. Not at you, at any rate. I think,' Janet said carefully, 'that she was angry with herself for letting things get so strained between your father and yourself. I take it you're an only child?'

'Yes. It seems to be a day for decisions and realisations.'

'What do you mean?' Angus asked.

'J-just that…well, I guess, if I'm honest with myself, I'll admit to the *real* reason Mick was interested in me. He said it often enough.'

'Said what?' Angus probed gently.

'That…' Stacey wiped at her eyes. 'That I should ask my dad for more…money. He'd only say it when he was waiting for his next student payment to come through and needed a fix.' She sniffed. 'I told him over and over that I wasn't talking to my dad and that money didn't matter to me.'

'What happened, Stacey?' Angus's tone was gently probing. 'Did he hit you?'

'No.' Stacey shook her head emphatically.

'Truthfully?'

The tears were flowing again and she slowly nodded. 'It was only when he needed a fix,' she sobbed. Janet held her close as Stacey once again faced another wound from her time with the disgusting Mick.

'I've been such an idiot,' she said between sobs.

'It doesn't matter what's happened in the past,' he said clearly, yet with compassion, 'with your parents, Mick, the drugs, the pregnancy—they no longer matter. What *does* matter is Madeline Jessica, your parents and you. You can make this work, Stacey. *You* can do it.'

Stacey wiped her eyes and smiled at Janet and Angus. 'You two...you must be guardian angels.' She blew her nose. 'I'd never have had the guts to face up to myself without you around. Thanks.'

She pulled the last tissue from the box.

'I'll get you some more,' Angus volunteered and left them alone.

Stacey gave Janet a watery smile. 'He's *so* nice. You're *so* lucky to have a guy like him.'

'Mmm,' Janet murmured, not at all sure what Stacey was getting at.

'It gives me hope that one day...one day I'll have someone who loves me just like you and Angus love each other.'

'Mmm,' Janet repeated.

'He told me that you've been friends for such a long time and that helps in your relationship.'

'He told you that, did he? What else did he tell you?'

Janet thought she must have had a weird expression on her face because Stacey quickly said, 'Oh he didn't tell me anything specific, Janet. Just that there's more to relationships than sex.'

Janet was surprised at Stacey's words. Considering the conversations they'd had about their mutual attraction, it wasn't something she'd have expected Angus to say.

'He's *so* cute. Anyone can see, by just *looking* at the two of you, that you're madly in love. You're lucky to have him.'

If only I could hold onto him, Janet said silently. Out loud she said, 'Yes. I'm very fortunate to have someone like him to lean on.' She purposely didn't comment on Stacey's misapprehension about them being in love. They had always loved each other in a family kind of way—even though Janet knew her own feelings were now of a more intimate nature.

The subject of their conversation returned with two boxes of tissues, and the two women smiled at each other, as though sharing a precious secret.

Janet wanted to see Cyril Montague before Stacey's mother arrived. That way she could devote her energies to helping the two women reconcile their differences. Although, if Jessica Wells's attitude on the phone was anything to go by, their meeting would run without a hitch.

Police Officer Shirmin came to take Stacey's statement of the previous night's events. He was pleased when Stacey agreed to press charges against Mick. He explained the procedure and the need for a court hearing, which Stacey acknowledged while nervously biting her fingernails. Next he obtained statements from both Angus and Janet before he finally left them in peace.

Pink came by to see Stacey and ordered her to sleep as her body was in desperate need of rest.

'That's our cue to visit Cyril Montague,' Angus announced as they left Stacey's room. They started walking down the corridor to the lifts.

'I thought I was doing the house call?'

'We only brought my car.'

'Are you saying I can't drive it? Don't you trust me?'

'Of course I trust you. Are you saying you don't want me to tag along? The sooner Cyril gets used to me the better.'

'Why? You'll be leaving in less than six months.' She stopped and turned to face him. 'I'm sorry, Angus. That was uncalled for.' She rubbed her brow. 'I guess the events of last night are beginning to catch up with me.'

'It's OK,' he said, and walked over to press the 'down' button for the lifts. 'It's better to take your fatigue out on me than anyone else. I know the *real* you, remember?'

'How could I forget?'

They were both silent on the drive to Cyril's house. When they arrived he wasn't on the porch as he usually was at this time of day. Prickles of apprehension spread through Janet's body as she knocked on the door.

At the same time they heard a loud crash, as though a glass had smashed. Janet knocked on the door again and called Cyril's name. There was another crash. She tried the handle but the door was locked.

Angus ran to the gate, which was unlocked and went around to the back of the house. 'Janet!' he called. She ran around to him, her black medical bag in hand. He was standing next to a window at the back of the house.

'The door is locked, the window is open. Let's go in.' Angus pulled out a pocket knife and slashed through the fly-screen, before pushing the window open wider and climbing through. They heard another crash.

'Hand me the bag,' he instructed, and left Janet to climb through.

They found Cyril in the kitchen, smashed glass on the floor around him. He was dressed in his pyjamas, his feet bare. He held a drinking glass in his hand, raised in the air.

'Wait...wait...' he was saying quietly. 'Now!' he called, and let the glass go. It smashed to the floor with the others. 'Bull's-eye—we've done it!'

'Cyril,' Janet said, and walked slowly towards him.

He turned his head sharply to look at her, his eyes wild with fear.

'The enemy,' he whispered with horror, and picked up another glass.

'No.' The word was firm and clear. 'I'm not the enemy...' She thought quickly for a moment. 'I'm your com-
manding officer. The attack has been a success and it's time
to head back to base.'

Angus picked up a kitchen chair and took it over to Cyril.
'Sit down and we'll drive you back to camp.'

Cyril sat on the chair. Angus lifted from the back and
Janet from the front, ensuring that Cyril's feet were well
clear of the floor. They crunched their way carefully
through the glass, thankful they were both wearing sensible
shoes, and into the living room. They lowered the chair.

'Here we are,' Janet soothed. 'Time for a rest.' They
manoeuvred him to his favourite chair and settled him in.
Cyril closed his eyes and was snoring within seconds.

'The cuts on his legs don't look too bad,' Angus said as
he took a closer look, 'but this one on his left foot will
need suturing.'

'I'll call an ambulance and Alister,' Janet said before the
two of them set to work, cleaning up. Janet vacuumed the
mess in the kitchen while Angus washed and dressed what
wounds he could. Cyril was now in a deep sleep, something
else that caused them concern.

'Was he in the war?'

'Not that I know of,' Janet answered. 'But Newcastle,
like the rest of the world, was affected by the war. Just
look at Fort Scratchley.'

'He has little bits of glass everywhere, Janet,' Angus said
when he was finished. 'I've done my best not to push them
in further and have managed to get a few out, but he'll
need to be monitored for quite a few days in hospital to
ensure none remain embedded.'

Alister arrived in a state of panic and rushed to his father's side.

'He's been sleeping like that for almost ten minutes. Out
cold,' Janet told Alister.

'Is…is that normal?' Alister asked.

'He's had an exhausting morning. It does mean that his mind isn't functioning quite as it used to. Alister, he can't live by himself any more,' Janet said softly. 'Most times, with dementia, the disease takes hold gradually, but in other instances the onset of symptoms can be accelerated. In your father's case, I'm afraid it's the latter.'

'When he gets to hospital I'll order another EEG and we can compare it with the first one,' Angus said.

'How long will Dad be in for?'

'At least four to five days. He may even need minor surgery to remove any slivers of glass which are buried but that would only require a local anaesthetic,' Angus answered.

'How do we get him to hospital now? I can put him in my car.' Alister looked around for his car keys.

'I've called an ambulance taxi,' Janet said as she picked up Alister's forgotten keys from the small table by the door. 'It's for non-urgent cases and, considering your father's health isn't in danger, he's not classified as an urgent case. It should be here soon, though.'

'You'll stay until then, won't you?' Alister asked, accepting the keys from Janet and putting them in his pocket.

'Of course we will. The only place Angus and I need to be today is back at the hospital with another patient. We'll be at the hospital to admit Cyril, before handing his care over to the staff. Promise me, though, if you have any questions or concerns you will call me.'

'Don't worry, Janet, I will.'

'You'll need to make arrangements for him to move in with you. Better that than a nursing home.'

'I want him with us for as long as we can. You've explained the ups and downs to us and at least we can get help with respite and other services that are available.

Leanne and I have both looked into things in great detail since we last spoke. We're ready.'

'Good, because it's time.' Janet gave Alister's hand a little squeeze. 'You'll all be fine.'

The ambulance pulled into the driveway, no sirens or lights flashing. Janet rode in the ambulance with Cyril while Angus and Alister followed in their own cars.

CHAPTER NINE

CYRIL didn't wake until they were wheeling him to his room. He sat upright before Janet and Alister were able to urge him back down. The orderly stopped wheeling the bed while they soothed a now very upset man.

'Everything's fine, Dad. It's me, Alister. I'm here.'

'Alister?' Cyril grasped wildly for his son's hand and Alister took his firmly.

'I'm here, Dad. It's all right. You've had a little accident and you're in hospital.'

'Hospital.' The fear in Cyril's voice reflected the terrified expression on his face. 'No. No. They'll never let me leave. I want to go home.'

He was starting to get very distressed and Janet asked the orderly to resume pushing the bed, trying to get Cyril to his room quickly to afford him some privacy.

'Cyril,' Janet said calmly, 'Alister is right. Once we get you sorted out, you can leave the hospital.'

'Don't let them put me in a home, son.'

'I wouldn't dare,' Alister replied with vehemence.

This news seemed to settle Cyril a little, although he didn't let go of his son's hand, even after they'd settled him in a private room.

'If having a bit of privacy helps Dad,' Alister had said when they'd arrived at the hospital and had been discussing room allocation, 'then the cost is irrelevant. We'll pay for the private room.'

Janet and Angus spoke with the doctors on the ward and Janet requested another EEG.

'We'll organise it for tomorrow when he's a bit more settled,' the ward doctor replied.

'Thanks. Would you mind contacting me when it's done? I'll be in some time during the afternoon.'

'No problem,' the doctor told her, and wrote it down in Cyril's notes.

They left Alister with his father and went to see how Stacey was progressing.

'I feel as though I'm living at this hospital at the moment,' Janet commented as they walked towards the maternity ward. 'Perhaps I should apply for a resident's room and get some sleep.'

'You are looking a little ruffled about the edges and you're starting to get black bags under your eyes.'

'Thank you *very* much, Angus.'

He chuckled at her words.

'Haven't you ever heard the saying, "If you can't say something nice, don't say anything at all"?'

'What about, "Honesty is the best policy"?'

She shook her head, not wanting to get into a discussion about honesty because she was certain that if Angus was honest with himself, he would admit that he loved her and would never leave her.

'Stacey should be fit for transfer some time later this afternoon and once she's gone, you can bet I'll be going home to get some sleep. First of all, let's see how she and her mother cope with being in the same room together.'

About that, Janet had no worries. When Jessica Wells arrived, she embraced her daughter so tightly that no one could doubt her sincerity. They left them alone to talk and sort things out before being properly introduced to Stacey's mother.

'I can't thank you enough for everything you've done for Stacey.'

'She's a strong young woman,' Angus commented. 'She and that beautiful baby of hers will do just fine.'

'Mum's promised to put herself in the firing line between Dad and myself, even though both of us will be trying hard to make it work.'

'Is he in Sydney?' Janet asked.

'He's overseas at the moment on business,' Jessica replied. 'He's due back in two weeks' time so that gives Stacey and me time to get things organised. I initially asked her to move back home, but the more we discussed it the more we both think it's appropriate that she and Madeline Jessica live on their own. That way, Kurt—that's my husband—won't be so inclined to interfere.'

'Although we'll be living in an apartment nice and close to home, it will still be our own.'

'Sounds like a brilliant idea. I'm sure the Wells women will be able to handle your father just wonderfully—especially Madeline. Little girls have a way of wrapping their grandfathers around their little fingers simply by looking at them.'

Jessica laughed. 'We'll be counting on it. She's already stolen her grandmother's heart.'

'She *is* beautiful, isn't she, Mum?'

'She's more than that,' Jessica said with tears in her eyes. 'She's an angel.' After wiping her eyes, Stacey's mother asked, 'How soon can we leave for Sydney? I want to be with both of my girls.'

Janet smiled. 'Once Stacey's been given the all-clear from Dr Pinkerton and Leesa, she can be transferred to Sydney. You'll still be in hospital for another week or so and you *must* rest and recuperate, otherwise you'll be no good to Maddy.'

'I promise,' Stacey said earnestly.

'I'll page those pesky doctors now,' Angus remarked. 'We need to get this family reunited.'

Once Stacey and her mother had made their farewells and been taken to the airport by ambulance taxi, Angus drove Janet home.

'Weren't you supposed to go out with Leesa tonight?' he asked as he turned the final corner and garaged the car.

'I told her I was too exhausted. She may be used to staying up all night and being on call but I'm not. I'll catch up with her another time.' She opened the car door and climbed out. 'Thanks for driving me home, Angus. I'm bushed. I'll see you later.'

Janet walked off, leaving Angus to lock his car. She heard him following her and turned abruptly to confront him. He didn't stop walking and they collided. Instinctively, his arms went around her waist to steady her while her hands pressed up against his chest.

'We have to stop meeting like this,' he drawled, before his head began to lower for a kiss.

'Please, Angus,' Janet whispered only moments before his lips touched hers. 'Don't.' The word was wrenched from her in agony. 'I can't keep doing this. I've told you my reasons why I can't be involved with you, yet at every possible opportunity you're kissing me.'

'I happen to like kissing you.' He smiled, one eyebrow raised in a roguish way.

'It's not the point. On Monday—in two days' time— you'll be heading off to New Zealand in search of another job.'

'That's who I am,' he offered by way of explanation.

'I know, and I…well, I accept that now. If you're not going to stay then I need to move on with my life, Angus.' She pulled herself from his grasp and felt the cool wind whip around her. 'I've advertised for a permanent partner.'

He crossed his arms. 'I see.'

Janet took offence at his posture. 'Don't you get all defensive on me, Angus O'Donnell. I offered you the job—a few times as I recall—and you turned me down. The fact remains that I still need a partner.'

'Of course,' he said, and shoved his hands into his trouser pockets. 'Just promise me one thing.'

'What?' She eyed him cautiously.

'Allow me to interview them with you.'

'I'm more than capable of—'

'I know you are but at least, with me being there, it will give you a slightly different perspective on your new male partner. Come on, Janet,' he pressed when she didn't reply. 'If I weren't here, I'm sure you'd ask Hamish to assist you in the screening process. We both know how busy he is so why don't you let me help? As a way of making up for leaving you in the lurch.'

'I'll think about it.' Janet turned away from him. 'Goodnight, Angus,' she threw over her shoulder, and unlocked her front door.

'Goodnight,' he replied.

It felt incredibly strange on Monday morning to arrive at the clinic and know that Angus wasn't there. Apart from the fact that she'd been trying to avoid him for the past few weeks, she had still been able to 'feel' his presence. Today…there was nothing.

'So this is how it'll be?' she asked herself as she read through her daily list of patients.

'Talking to yourself again?' Karen asked as she walked in.

'A sign of old age, or so I'm told,' Janet replied. 'I have my list so when the masses start arriving send them in.'

'Will do,' Karen acknowledged.

Janet had started off down the corridor before Karen called out, 'Oh, how did Friday go? At the university.'

Janet took a few steps backwards and stood in the corridor. 'Friday? I can't remember back that far—it was a hectic weekend.'

'Why don't you tell me about it while I make some coffee? Mrs Hay is your first patient and she's not due to arrive for another fifteen minutes.'

So the two women sat in the kitchen and talked. 'Sounds as though you spent most of Saturday at the hospital,' Karen remarked when Janet had finished. 'I'll pull Cyril Montague's file for you so you can make some notes.'

'Thanks.' Janet took her cup to the sink and washed it. 'Also, I've advertised for a permanent partner, so if there are any calls about that put them through to me.'

'What about Angus?' Karen asked with surprise. 'I thought, well, that you two were...' She didn't finish her sentence. 'Have you offered him the job?'

'Several times. Each time he's rejected it.'

'That doesn't mean he's rejected *you*.'

'Yes, it does.' Janet shook her head sadly. 'Angus doesn't want to put down roots.'

'So what's stopping you from having "an affair to remember," as they say.'

'It's just not me.'

Karen gave her a long, hard look. 'You're hopelessly in love with him, aren't you?'

'Am I that obvious?'

'Wow! You mean I'm *right*. I was just probing. Wow! So you're in love with Angus.'

'A lot of good it's doing me.'

'Have you told him?'

'It wouldn't make a scrap of difference. Angus feels he can't stay. Believe me, I've tried to change his mind but he says he can't. Which is why he's gone to New Zealand.'

'I thought he was going to speak at a conference?'

'He is, but he's most likely searching for another six-month locum position for when this one is finished.'

'I see.' Karen's tone was a bit dejected. 'So he's definitely leaving.' It was a statement, not a question.

'Yes.' The bell over the front door tinkled. 'That will be Mrs Hay to have her blood pressure checked. Tell her to come on through,' Janet said, and went to her consulting room.

The rest of the week passed very slowly for Janet. Angus had burst into her life and turned it upside down so quickly that she could hardly believe it. Even though he would soon return, it was a bitter and lonely foretaste of what she could expect when he left for good just after Christmas.

''Tis better to have loved and lost than never to have loved at all,' she told her reflection on the day he was due back. Perhaps if she gave in to his suggestion to take what they could, while they could, she might—just might—be able to persuade him to stay. The more she thought about it, the more she knew she'd just be setting herself up for an even bigger fall.

She didn't want Angus to stay solely because of her—that would have been selfish. She loved him so much that his true happiness was of paramount importance to her. If he felt stifled and closed in by not moving around every six months, she knew he'd come to resent her.

The way things stood was best for both of them. 'Friends,' she said, and pasted on a smile. He would be back this evening and she wasn't sure what to do. Should she go to the airport to meet him? Invite some friends over for dinner or maybe a quiet dinner for two?

The issue was taken out of her hands when he turned up at half past three at the clinic. He strode into her consulting room, swivelled her chair around so she was facing him and planted a big kiss on her lips.

'I did it,' he said triumphantly.

Janet tried to smile. 'That's great, Angus.' She stood and pushed past him. 'I'm happy for you.' She stared out of the window, her back to him.

'Happy? That's it? You're happy for me? I win the award for best paper at the conference and all you can say is that you're *happy* for me? Janet, we need to work on your vocabulary.'

Janet spun around. 'Oh, the award for best paper—of course. Congratulations, Angus, although I'm sure you deserved it. You're a brilliant doctor.'

'That's more like it.' His face still radiated excitement and Janet's heart lurched at the smile that could melt any barriers she erected between them. 'I managed to catch an earlier flight. I couldn't wait to tell you.'

'You couldn't?' she asked, a little surprised. 'Well, I'm…I'm flattered.'

'Who else understands me the way you do?'

'I… Well… I don't—'

'I wish you could have been there with me, Janet. It was so exciting. I'd already won the award for the general practitioner category but to win overall—above all those specialists. It's not just a win for me, it's a win for all general practitioners.'

'I'm sure it is.' His mood was infectious and Janet's smile began to match his.

He picked her up and spun her around the room.

'Put me down.' She laughed and finally he complied.

'We should celebrate. I'll call Hamish and Leesa to see if they're available as this is one piece of good news I'd like to rub in my brother's face—in a non-threatening kind of way, of course.'

'Of course,' Janet agreed.

He looked down at her, his blue eyes still alive with excitement. 'When I'm with you, there's no need for polite pretence about the award. I'm so darned proud of myself but I don't have to be reserved in that pride around you.' His gaze sobered and he reached out a hand to draw her closer. 'I missed you, Janet.'

They were four words she'd thought she'd never hear from Angus's lips but here they were and he'd actually said them. As far as she'd been concerned, Angus never missed anyone. His mouth swooped hungrily down on to hers and Janet staggered back from the impact. His arm encircled her waist, steadying her.

He kissed her so passionately, so completely—so lovingly—that for one brief moment Janet thought everything might work out all right between them.

When he raised his head he gazed down into her face. 'You feel and taste so good.'

Janet could only smile at his words. There was no way she was going to tell him how she felt because she was terrified she'd scare him away. She still had several questions to ask him, top of the list being about the next locum job he'd lined up.

The buzzer on her intercom sounded and Karen's voice said, 'Mr Deers is here.'

Janet broke from their embrace and walked over to her desk. She pressed the button. 'Send him through, thank you.'

'Right, I'll let you get back to work and go and call my brother with the news.' He walked to the door then stopped and looked at her again. 'Will you try to finish close to time? We have a lot of celebrating to do.'

'I'll do my best—*if* you stop interrupting me.'

'Sorry.' He held his hands up in self-defence. 'I'm going now.'

'It's wonderful news, Angus,' she added before he closed the door.

When Mr Deers came through, Janet found it difficult to

school her thoughts and give the thirty-two-year-old primary school teacher her undivided attention.

She was sure he was going to scold her for behaving like a silly schoolgirl because that was exactly how she felt. One kiss from Angus and she was floating on cloud nine once more, without a care for anyone or anything else.

Angus went to his consulting room and shut the door. Picking up the phone, he dialled the hospital and waited to be put through to Hamish's clinic.

'Welcome back. I can only spare a few minutes. How did things go?' Hamish asked.

Angus told Hamish about winning the award and received hearty congratulations from his brother.

'What about the company? Did you have a meeting with them?' Hamish asked.

'Yes. They're doing everything they can to terminate the contract without any penalties being incurred. I've consented to stay until they find someone to replace me but I don't know how long that will take.'

'Can you stall Janet on the partnership issue?'

'I don't think that's fair to her. I can't tell her what's happening and they may not find a replacement for another six to eight months. Not everyone likes to spy on their colleagues, Hamish. I've been doing it for just under eight years and it's definitely time for a change.'

'There's more to your relationship with Janet than just a partnership, isn't there?' Hamish asked.

'Yes.'

'Don't break her heart, Angus.' There was a small hint of warning in Hamish's tone.

'I don't intend to,' his brother answered.

That night they all went out to dinner to celebrate Angus's award. Hamish was very proud of his younger brother and Leesa lavished praise on him.

Angus sat close to Janet and she could feel the warmth of his thigh pressing against the smooth linen of her dress. When they were enjoying their coffee, he casually draped his arm across the back of her chair, indicating there was a lot more going on between them than there really was.

Janet was beginning to wonder at his behaviour, especially on the drive back to the house. He held her hand the entire way, except when he stopped the car and insisted she stay where she was so he could open the door for her.

'Thank you,' she said as he helped her out of the car. 'I've had such a wonderful evening, Angus.'

'Would you like to come inside?' His eyes seemed alive with desire and Janet felt herself being drawn under his spell.

'Uh… I'd…I'd better…not,' she said uncertainly. 'I… don't think it would be wise.'

'Who is it that you don't trust, Janet? Me or yourself?'

'A bit of both,' she confessed.

'Just come in for a cup of tea and talk. I promise.' He crossed his heart. 'Please?' That final word was her undoing.

'All right,' she capitulated. 'One cup and then I need to get some rest. Cyril's coming out of hospital tomorrow and moving into Alister's home. I want to be there for him.'

'How has he been doing in the last week?'

'He's been holding his own. The EEG showed a further abnormality when compared with his earlier scan. He's accepted—slowly—that he'll not be moving back into his house. It's been a difficult week but he has good support from his family.'

'Speaking of families, have you heard from Stacey?' Angus plugged in the kettle and moved around the kitchen, pulling out the tea things.

'Didn't you see the flowers in the waiting room? They're

huge!' Janet perched herself on a bench stool and watched him.

'I must have missed them on my mad dash to your consulting room. Are they nice?'

'Beautiful. Karen had to split them up into several vases. They arrived on Wednesday but even today—two days later—they still look and smell fresh. Stacey wrote a note with them, saying that she was recovering well in hospital and that Maddy was slowly gaining weight. Apparently, Jessica has moved into the hospital as well, refusing to leave her daughter's and granddaughter's side.'

Angus smiled. 'Ah, families—ya gotta love 'em.'

'Have you called your parents to tell them your good news?'

'Not yet,' he replied, glancing quickly at the clock. 'The time zones are wrong. I'll call them later.'

'So, tell me all about New Zealand,' she prompted, ensuring there wasn't an awkward silence between them. Even if she heard something she didn't like, it was better than them gazing into each other's eyes because she knew she'd have a very hard time resisting—she always did.

He told her all about the conference and the other papers which had been presented.

'Did you meet up with your...friend?'

'What friend?' he asked with a frown as he poured them both another cup of tea.

'The one who might find you another job.' The words were said with complete nonchalance—or, at least, Janet hoped they were. Angus knew she didn't want him to go but she also wanted him to know that she respected his decision and wanted only happiness for him.

As far as *she* was concerned, he needed to look no further than herself if it was *true* happiness he was searching for.

'Oh, *that* friend. Yes, I did catch up with him.'

'And?'

'We talked. There are some developments in the pipeline and I just have to wait and see how they pan out. Hopefully, things will go my way. He'll get back to me later. Besides, I've still got a few more months here.'

'True,' Janet said with a sigh of relief. Nothing was definite. Surely that was a good sign?

'What about you? Did anything…untoward happen while I was away?'

'No.'

'What about your plans for finding a permanent partner?'

It was as though he could read her mind. Janet shuddered involuntarily and took a sip of her tea. 'As I've told you, I've advertised,' was all she said.

'And,' he prompted.

'I've had three replies.'

'When are you planning to interview?'

'Next week. Two on Wednesday and one on Friday.'

'What time? I'll make sure I keep it free.'

'Excuse me, Angus, but as I've mentioned before I'm more than capable of interviewing for a new partner by myself.'

'I'm not saying you're not capable, Janet. I'm merely saying it's always good to have a second opinion. Regardless of what the résumé tells you, it's not the way to decide about a partnership. These things take time.'

'Thank you very much.' Janet placed her cup back on the bench and stood. 'How low your opinion of me must be, Angus, because, regardless of what you think, I'm not completely brainless. When I advertised I stated that it was a six-month position with the possibility of a partnership in the future. *Possibility.* I'd never sign anyone on as a partner unless I was absolutely sure. And, yes, when it came down to that final decision, I would ask Hamish *and* Leesa for their advice.'

'But not me.'

'*You won't be here!*' she all but yelled at him. How dared he…? Janet was so angry she couldn't even *think* of words to describe him.

'Mr I-can't-handle-responsibility-so-I'll-move-on-while-I-can will be in another country by then.' She collected her bag and coat. 'I've offered you this partnership countless times and each time you've turned it down. As far as our professional relationship goes, you are here until the end of the year. Then you'll vanish again. I don't need your help with the interviews for a partner I'm more than capable of choosing myself. *I'm* the one who'll be working with him, not *you.*' She stalked to the door and turned to face him. The gaze she levelled at him was icy. 'Thank you for your offer, Angus,' she said with a bit more decorum. 'I decline.'

With that, Janet opened the door and walked out.

Angus watched her go, part of him wanting to run after her. To tell her that he'd stay—*anything* to stop her from being angry with him.

Instead, he closed the door she'd left open and began to tidy up. What was it about her that made him lose all rational thought? During the entire time he'd spent in New Zealand, all he'd thought about had been her. He'd wanted her to have been with him as he'd listened to new and innovative approaches to a variety of specialities. He'd wanted her with him as he'd done some sightseeing during his free time. He'd wanted her with him as he'd been presented with that award. But most of all he'd wanted her with him all night long.

Angus turned out the light and walked to his bedroom, setting his alarm to wake him in time to call his mother.

When the alarm sounded, he wearily reached out a hand, lifted the telephone receiver and pressed the preset phone

number for his parents. With his eyes still closed, he waited
to be connected. Sean O'Donnell answered the phone.

'Hi, Dad,' Angus said into the receiver, before holding
it away from his ear as his father's joy at hearing from his
youngest son boomed down the line. A smile crossed
Angus's face. He'd missed his parents.

'Your mother's here, son. She's almost ripping the phone
out of my hand she's so eager to talk to y...' His father's
words trailed away into the distance.

'Angus? Oh, darling, it's so wonderful to hear from you.'

The obvious delight in Mary's voice made Angus happy.

They chatted for a while then she said, 'I presume there's
a reason for your call? You can't be phoning Egypt in the
early hours of the morning in Australia simply to make idle
chit-chat with your parents.'

'As a matter of fact, I do have some good news.' He
told her about the conference and the award, before listening to her praise her brilliant son.

'So where is my genius off to next? Some remote island
the tourists have never heard of to bring good health to all
the natives?'

'Ah, no. Actually, I'm still deciding.'

Mary was silent for a moment. 'That isn't like you. Is
everything all right, dear?'

'Everything's fine, Mum.'

'You and Janet aren't having any difficulties, are you?
Because let me tell you, Angus O'Donnell, that Janet
Stevenson is a very special woman. You be on your best
behaviour.'

'Mum—Mum! Calm down. I just have a few options to
weigh up before I decide.'

'Well, at least we instilled *that* in you. Just make sure
you have all the facts before making your decision.'

All the facts. Of one fact Angus was certain. His longing
for Janet to be with him in New Zealand had been a shock

to his system. He'd never felt that way about a woman before. He'd always been able to separate business and pleasure, but with Janet... He felt as though he were in no man's land.

'What? Sorry, Mum. What did you say?'

Mary tut-tutted. 'You're spending a fortune, calling me, and then don't listen to a word I say. You must be preoccupied and, if I know you, it'll be a woman who's interfering in this conversation.'

He gave a nervous laugh. 'What makes you say that?'

'Angus, *please.* I'm your mother, darling. Give me a little credit. So, who is she?'

'Mum.' The word was said softly but held an underlying tone that she was about to cross the invisible line children often drew between themselves and their parents.

'All right. We'll meet her soon enough. At least she seems to be making you think things through a bit more.'

'What's that supposed to mean?'

'The fact that you're not firmly decided on leaving Newcastle. I know I've nagged you for years about settling down, but that's my job—I'm your mother and I'm the only one you have. All this jet-setting about the world was what you once needed, but do you really need it now? Is it really all that important to you? Haven't your priorities changed since being back in your home town and renewing old acquaintances?'

For a brief moment Angus thought his mother could read his thoughts. Did she know what had happened between himself and Janet? Had Janet said something to her mother who had in turn said something to his mother? All he knew was that he hadn't heard the calm and re-assuring tone his mother was now using for quite a while.

'I think,' he said after a long pause—one she didn't interrupt, 'that my priorities have changed.'

CHAPTER TEN

'I SAID I didn't want you to be here,' Janet reiterated to Angus. They'd been avoiding each other and only speaking in polite monosyllables whenever they did happen to bump into each other—after all, the consulting rooms weren't all that large.

'I know what you said and I respect that, but the fact remains that an applicant feels more intimidated when there's an interviewing panel of more than one. Come on, Janet. I'll be on my best professional behaviour,' he said, giving her his winning smile. Janet tried her hardest to resist but, considering she hadn't seen his smile for five whole days, she succumbed quite quickly, much to her disgust.

'All right.' She didn't smile at him, didn't add any pleasantries. She wanted him to know that she was still mad at him but, nevertheless, what he'd said made sense.

They walked into her consulting room which was where the interviews were to take place. She pulled a chair around the desk for him and they sat down, waiting for Karen to show the first applicant through.

After an hour of questions, Janet said, 'Thank you very much for your time, Ian.' She held out her hand and smiled. He shook hers and then Angus's before walking to the door.

When it closed behind him Angus said, 'He's not right for the job.'

Janet seemed surprised. 'I thought he was quite good. He handled your inquisition well.'

'He'll buckle under pressure. If you have emergency situations, such as Mr Campbell having a heart attack in the

waiting room, I'll bet you every cent I have that Dr Ian...'
Angus searched the page for the applicant's surname
'...Merribore won't be able to handle it.'

'Fine,' Janet said and sat down to make some notes.

'Fine what? You accept my opinion?' Angus seemed surprised at her acquiescence.

'No. Fine, I'll take that bet. I'm just making a note of it
now.'

Karen pressed the buzzer and let them know the next
applicant had arrived.

Angus shuffled his papers about. 'A Dr Jon Stuart. Right,
let's see if he has more to offer.'

An hour and a half later Dr Stuart left the room.

'He's not right either.'

'How?'

'You mean you can't see it? Then it's a good thing I
insisted on helping you.'

'Oh, please.' Janet rolled her eyes. 'It doesn't matter who
I interview, I doubt whether anyone would measure up to
be as brilliant as you, Angus, but need I remind you yet
again that you've turned this job down? If you're unable
to make an impartial decision, I'll interview the third applicant by myself.'

'When is he scheduled for an interview?'

'This Friday. I'm driving up to Nelson's Bay to see him.'

'Excuse me?' Angus raised an eyebrow in disbelief.
'*You're* driving to see *him*?'

'Yes. He's completely snowed under and when he suggested I go up there I thought...why not? I haven't been
to the Bay for quite a while and I've always loved it there.
I feel...' She sighed. 'At peace.'

'Fine. Then we'll go on Friday. What time?'

'*I'm* leaving here at six. I've spoken with Karen and
she's marked it in the book so I don't run overtime.'

'That'll mean you're there at dinnertime.'

'Precisely. Dr McNeil suggested we conduct the interview over dinner. Apparently, they've opened a new Chinese restaurant on the foreshore and the food is rumoured to be delicious.'

'Dinner? He's asked you to dinner? Doesn't that tell you what sort of man he is straight off? For crying out loud, Janet, are you *that* thick? You don't know anything about this man yet here you are, driving an hour to Nelson's Bay—at night-time—and having dinner with him while you interview him about a partnership.'

Janet simply shrugged. 'You're making a mountain out of a molehill, Angus.'

'I'm…what?' he spluttered. 'It's just as well I came back. Hamish is so busy at the hospital and helping Leesa study that you're lucky I'm here to look out for you.'

'So I guess that means you're coming,' Janet stated, and gathered up her papers. She put them into her briefcase, before reaching for her coat.

'You bet I'm coming.'

'Fine. We'll take my car, and if you're not ready to leave by six I'll go without you.' With that, she walked out of her consulting room, leaving him spluttering silently to himself.

Janet said a cheery goodnight to Karen, before walking home. She knew Angus would catch up with her in a few minutes so she took the time to congratulate herself on handling the situation brilliantly.

On the drive up to Nelson's Bay Janet remained in a good humour. Angus had been set to be all 'big brotherly', but after the first twenty minutes of lecturing her and realising he was getting nowhere he stopped.

They slipped easily into conversation after that and soon they were driving through Nelson's Bay. Janet followed the directions Dr Andrew McNeil had given her to the restaurant and found it with ease.

'One point for Dr McNeil. He's clear in his directions.'

Angus looked at her. 'If you don't mind, I'll reserve my judgement until all the facts are in.'

'As will I,' she said solemnly, and set off into the restaurant, leaving him to follow.

'What name, please?' the waiter asked.

'McNeil,' Janet said as Angus walked in.

'Right this way, please.'

They were led to a large table in the busy restaurant. Judging by the number of people that packed the room, the food must be incredible, Janet thought.

The waiter left them at a table with a small bow. A man stood and held out his hand. 'I'm Andrew McNeil. You must be Dr Stevenson.' He was probably a little shorter than Angus and looked to be in his early fifties. His hair was greying at the temples and his brown eyes were twinkling with the smile that was on his lips.

'Please, call me Janet.'

'This is my wife, Audrey.'

Janet shook her hand, before introducing Angus. The look of sheer shock on his face was only fleeting but it was one that Janet thoroughly enjoyed.

'Pleased to meet you Audrey,' he said. 'I was only expecting to meet your husband, but considering we run a family practice, it's good to meet Andrew's family.'

'Smooth talker,' Janet mumbled as they sat down. Angus simply turned and gave her a smile.

'We have two teenage children,' Audrey commented, returning his smile, 'but there was no way we could drag them here. They're embarrassed to be seen in public with us,' she said in a stage whisper.

'I remember that time of my life well.' Angus laughed.

'We're looking forward to them outgrowing it,' Andrew

added. 'It's one of the main reasons we've decided to move back to Newcastle, hence my application for this locum position.'

'The kids,' Audrey explained. 'They want more of a social scene. We know it's a strange time for Andrew to sell his practice here and move, but the children's happiness is important to both of us.'

Over a banquet of the most delicious Chinese food Janet had ever eaten, the four of them talked like old friends. She was certain that even Angus couldn't find fault with Andrew.

'We've had a lovely evening,' Angus remarked some time later as he shook hands with the McNeils.

'We'll let you know some time next week about the position,' Janet said with a smile, certain she'd found the second best partner in the world. Angus, of course, was still her first choice.

'I'm still fairly busy here,' Andrew confessed, 'so if you're having trouble getting hold of me, give Audrey a call at home.'

'Right. I have all your numbers so I'll track you down one way or another.'

'I'd just like to say,' Andrew added as he took his wife's hand in his, 'that, regardless of the outcome, we've really enjoyed ourselves this evening and wouldn't mind keeping in touch.'

'I'd like that,' Janet responded honestly.

'We'd better get going, Janet, or we'll be late for house calls tomorrow,' Angus said.

'I know the story all too well,' Andrew said with a nod of his head. 'Drive carefully.'

They left the McNeils and walked back to Janet's car. She waited until they were seated, before saying, 'So go on. Do your worst. Find fault with Andrew McNeil.'

Angus was silent for a moment, before shaking his head. 'I can't,' he said softly. 'He'd be perfect for the job.'

With those words Angus effectively severed the dream Janet had been holding onto. Now he was giving her his blessing to hire another doctor to take his place. He would leave and Andrew McNeil and his family would become a part of her business. It was so…final.

Janet reached out a hand to start the engine and realised that she was suddenly very tired. Tired of trying to read Angus's expressions. Tired of having to decipher her own emotions and tired of trying to win the man she loved when he so clearly didn't love her. If he did, he'd stay.

'Something wrong?' he asked when her hand stilled on the ignition key.

'Yes. Actually, would you mind driving? I'm rather tired.' She unbuckled her seat belt and quickly climbed out of the car before he could ask any questions. She walked slowly around the car in the opposite direction to Angus, climbing into the passenger seat and buckling her seat belt.

'Thanks,' she said, turning her head to look out of the window.

Very little was said between them for the next twenty minutes. Traffic heading back to Newcastle wasn't heavy but the oncoming traffic was. It seemed as though half of the population of Newcastle would be spending their week-end at Nelson's Bay.

A few of the cars that passed them were speeding and Janet's thoughts about her personal life were put on hold.

'I can't believe the speeds some of these people are travelling at.' She shook her head in disgust.

'You read my mind,' Angus replied, not once taking his eyes off the road. As if on cue, a red car swerved around the corner. The sound of screeching tyres pierced the air at the driver's obvious attempts to gain control of the vehicle.

Angus braked hard and Janet looked behind them, thankful there weren't any other cars coming.

As though in slow motion, the red car flipped up on two wheels before gravity forced it to roll. Janet watched in horror as the car rolled onto their side of the road, then off the bitumen and slammed side on into an old gum-tree which had been there for many years. Its thick trunk stopped the vortex of red, the car now a crumpled mess.

Angus braked harder and pulled off the road. The instant their car had stopped, both of them sprang out and Janet snatched for her medical bag.

Angus reached the wreckage first while Janet called the emergency numbers from her mobile phone.

'Can you see anyone?' she called as Angus was peering through the front windshield.

'I need a strong torch,' he said, and she quickly flipped open her bag and handed him one. 'There's hardly any windscreen.' Angus edged closer and shone the torch around. 'There's no one in the car so they must have been thrown out.'

'It smells like the fuel tank's been ruptured,' Janet remarked as they both backed away. She only had one really strong torch so she stood with Angus as he guided the beam in a slow, sweeping motion.

'Back there,' Janet pointed to where he'd just passed. They moved closer, the grass at their feet becoming longer the further they proceeded into the scrub around them.

'Good spotting,' Angus commended her as they ran carefully towards the driver. When they reached him Janet started on neuro-vascular observations while Angus checked his bones for breakage.

'Pulse is very weak and breathing is shallow,' she reported.

'Internal bleeding and possible punctured lung,' Angus surmised.

She reached for her small medical torch and checked the man's pupils. 'Pupils responding to light. Angus, his breath stinks of stale beer.'

'Driving under the influence. Doesn't pay, does it?' He ran his hands over the man's left arm, feeling carefully for breakages. 'I know I'm no orthopaedic surgeon, but it feels as though he's broken every bone in his body.' Angus glanced up at her. 'Do you have a portable stretcher in the car?'

'No.' She thought fast. 'All I have is a space blanket.'

'Get it. We need to move both him and us away from the car. If it explodes, I don't want to be anywhere near it.'

Janet ran back to her car to fetch the blanket, mentally urging the ambulance and police to hurry up and reach their position. When she'd called for the ambulance she'd asked for the details to be passed to both police and fire personnel, as was common practice for motor vehicle accidents. Although, if that car did explode, she thought as she made her way back, they'd need more than one fire crew. The land surrounding them was a definite fire hazard and if the wind continued to pick up there'd be no telling what might happen.

A shudder ripped through her. She also knew that if Angus hadn't braked hard when he'd first seen the speeding car come around the corner, they wouldn't have been here, helping the occupant. Where the red car had rolled onto their side of the road, it would have connected with her car and crushed them both like sardines in a can.

'Any change in his situation?' she asked as she knelt beside Angus again.

'No. Let's spread the blanket out and move him to safety.' They unfolded the blanket, its silver colour glinting in the torchlight. 'Usual procedure for moving a patient,' he instructed Janet, and she gave him a nod.

As carefully as they could, they moved the injured man. 'We need to move fast.'

They each held two corners of the blanket and, on the count of three, lifted their patient off the ground.

'Keep him as low as possible. Good.' Angus's voice was calm as he followed in Janet's footsteps. She had her back to him so she could see where she was going and led them via the path she'd taken before. There were several small shrubs in the way but they negotiated them as best they could.

'Set him down slowly. Easy…easy,' Angus instructed when they reached her car. 'Good. Let's do those observations again.'

By the time Janet had finished taking their patient's pulse again, she could hear the wail of sirens.

'At last,' she whispered. 'His pulse is weaker than before. I don't know if he'll make it.'

The ambulance pulled up near their car. The police and fire personnel weren't too far behind and soon Janet and Angus were answering questions left, right and centre.

'That car is very unstable,' the chief firefighter reported. 'We'll douse it before it has a chance to explode.'

Janet watched as the firemen set to work, reeling out the hose. She watched the chief give the signal to turn the water on but at that instant a loud explosion filled the air and a huge ball of orange and red fire blinded them. She felt the ground tremble beneath her and shrank away from the sight.

She felt a comforting arm around her shoulders and she cowered into it.

'It's all right,' Angus said in her ear. 'The cavalry is here.'

The firemen were in action, their water extinguishing the flames before they could do more damage.

'Just as well you took the risk to move the patient,' one

of the attending police officers remarked to them. 'We'd all be toast if you hadn't.'

When the patient was ready to go, Janet and Angus followed the ambulance to Newcastle General where they answered even more questions. Hamish and Leesa were both on call that night but the patient's first priority was to have the internal bleeding controlled, as well as his lung which turned out to be punctured.

'There's not much else you can do at this stage,' Hamish told them both. 'Take Janet home and make sure she gets some rest,' he instructed his younger brother. 'She looks as though she's at the end of her tether.'

'Call us if anything happens,' he told Hamish, who nodded.

Angus placed a protective arm around Janet's shoulders and ushered her out of the hospital.

'You OK?' he asked as she sat in the passenger seat.

'No,' she whispered. 'Just take me home…please.'

Angus shut her door and walked around to the driver's side. After securing both his and Janet's seat belt, he tuned the radio to a classical-music station and drove through the city streets.

When they arrived home, Janet was still looking aimlessly out of the window.

'We're here,' Angus said. When she didn't move, he undid her seat belt and came around the car to help her out. Janet managed to walk inside and into the lounge room where she gratefully collapsed, the soft cushions enveloping her.

'Would you like a cup of tea? Coffee?'

Janet shook her head. She looked up and met his eyes. 'Just…hold me.' She'd whispered the last two words. Angus didn't need to be told twice and sat down beside her, gathering her securely into his arms.

They sat there for a good ten minutes. There were no

lights on, just the warmth of the gas heater Angus had switched on.

'Talk to me, Janet,' he urged quietly.

She sighed with anguish. 'On two separate occasions to-night, we were nearly killed.' Janet could feel the tears prickling behind her eyes. 'If you hadn't initially braked when you did, his car would have crushed ours. And if we hadn't moved him that car would have exploded and... and...' She broke off on a sob and buried her face in Angus's chest.

'Shh. I know. It's all right, Janet. Shh,' he repeated, and held her tighter. When her tears were spent, Janet sat back and looked into his eyes. She loved him so much.

'This entire night has simply reinforced how fragile human life really is. Angus, I don't want you to feel trapped by what I'm about to say but I don't want another moment to pass by without telling you how I truly feel.' She looked at his mouth and then back into his eyes. Her heart was hammering forcefully in her chest and her breathing increased with nervousness. 'I... Well...I love you.'

She watched a smile spread over his face and continued quickly, 'That's the reason I've been so reluctant to get involved with you.'

'Because you *love* me.' He nodded slowly. 'That's why you kept harping on about me only staying for six months.'

'I didn't *harp,*' she countered quickly, her nervousness disappearing to be replaced by annoyance.

'I know. I was just teasing.' His smile was now brilliant and he bent his head to kiss her lips. It was a gentle, re-assuring kiss but at the same time very possessive. 'There's something I need to tell you,' he said when he'd rasied his head. 'It may be a breach of contract but, considering what you've just confessed—that you love me—I feel I owe you more of an explanation than I've previously given.'

Janet waited eagerly for what he had to say, her hands held firmly in his own.

'The…company that I've been contracted to for nearly eight years is a pharmaceutical firm. You know how they give out money for research grants and clinical trials?'

Janet nodded, her brow slightly furrowed at his words. This was the last thing she'd expected him to say. A pharmaceutical company!

'Good. Well, they hire people—GPs, other researchers. People who can get close to the candidates who have received money from the company—who won't arouse too much suspicion—to investigate the research. My job has been to ensure the funds are being properly distributed and that clinical trial records aren't falsified in any way.'

'But why are you here in Newcastle?' Janet's tone was immediately defensive. '*I'm* not involved in any research.'

'There's been a bit of a lull in recipients for investigation. They informed me of a candidate in New Zealand but couldn't place me there until the end of this year. That left a six-month gap in my schedule so, instead of remaining idle, I decided to take the opportunity to come home and catch up with my family. When I mentioned it to Hamish, he told me you were looking for someone and it all fell into place.' He kissed the tip of her nose. 'I doubt anyone— especially you and I—could have predicted the sexual attraction we feel for each other.'

'I know it took *me* by surprise.' Janet smiled, feeling more calm than she had all day long. He *wasn't* an emotional nomad, as she'd previously accused him. He'd been investigating research frauds and *that* was the reason he'd moved around so much.

'Why didn't you tell me before about this company?'

'I have a confidentiality clause in my contract. The only person who knows what I do, apart from the company, is—'

'Hamish,' she finished with a nod. 'Why doesn't that surprise me?'

'He only knows because I discussed everything with him when I was offered the job.'

'When did all this happen?'

'Remember I told you about my first job overseas—with the woman who extended my contract and then dumped me after a few more months?'

Janet nodded.

'She was a recipient of a research grant and I'd accidentally stumbled across some accounting records she'd falsified. When I reported it to the company, she fired me. Two weeks later the company hired me on a contract basis to report any inconsistencies to them. They're the reason I've moved around so much and six months is a decent time frame to uncover any wrongdoings.'

'Sounds dangerous.'

'It's not. Not really,' he clarified. 'It's all presented in the form of a report and then I move on. End of story.'

'So you're a super-sleuth.'

'Something like that.' He smiled.

'And your next job is in New Zealand?'

'Yes.' He raised her hand to his lips and kissed it. 'I contacted the company and met their representatives while I was in New Zealand to try and terminate my contract.'

Janet's eyes widened with surprise. 'W-why? Why would you want to do that?' Her heartbeat, which had returned to its regular rhythm, started to pick up the pace again.

'Because of you,' he whispered, and placed a fleeting kiss on her lips. 'You have single-handedly turned my world upside down. I can't function without you, Janet. I need you in my life.'

Janet was utterly speechless for a moment, amazed that

he would give everything up to be with her. Her expression
changed and she frowned once more.

'If you wanted to be with me, why did you give the OK
to Andrew McNeil? I mean, if you're going to terminate
your contract with this company, you can accept the partnership with me. Unless,' she added quickly, 'you'd rather
not continue working with me.'

'Janet.' He squeezed her hands. 'I love working alongside you and would give anything to make it so, but a
condition of my termination is for them to find a replacement. It may take a day, a week or a month. I have no idea
when they'll be able to engage someone they can trust. It's
not the sort of position you can advertise in the paper.

'I don't want you to be left in the lurch in case I *do* need
to go to New Zealand at the end of this six-month position.
Andrew McNeil is a good doctor and would be perfect for
the practice. Besides, if I stayed, I'd also want to do the
university lecturing Leesa told me about—perhaps even apply for a research grant myself. The company owes me *that*
much, at least.'

Janet closed her eyes momentarily, her head beginning
to ache from fatigue. 'I'm so confused but one thing I know
for certain, Angus, is that I can't live without you.'

Angus kissed her closed eyelids and pulled her closer to
him. Janet snuggled in again, refusing to think any more
about anything.

'Just relax, darling,' he whispered, and kissed the top of
her head. A warm feeling of contentedness settled over her
at his endearment.

'Hello?' A distant voice broke through Janet's hazy dream.
'Hello? Janet?' It was her mother calling.

Janet mumbled as the dream started to disappear—and
what a beautiful dream it had been. She'd been wrapped in

Angus's loving arms all night long and all was right with her world. She loved him and that was all that mattered.

Love! The thought brought her brain instantly back on line and her eyes snapped open. The next thing she realised was that she wasn't at all comfortable. She moved slightly and realised she was lying on something. No. Not just something but someone. Angus!

The knock at the door became louder. 'Janet? Hell-o-o?' her mother's voice carolled. 'Wake up, sleepyhead.'

There was no time for thought. Janet broke free from Angus's arms which were wrapped around her. 'Angus! Wake up.' She glanced at the clock on the wall. 'Half past ten!'

'Janet?' he said sleepily, and stretched languorously. He opened his eyes and looked into hers briefly before he smiled slowly. 'Good morning, darling.'

'Not now, Angus.' Janet scrambled off the lounge. 'My mother is here.'

'There's no reply at Angus's house either,' another female voice said. Angus's eyes snapped open as well.

'Mum?' He stood beside Janet. 'What are they doing here?' he whispered.

'I don't know but they can't find us like this. Think, Janet, think,' she muttered. 'Maybe we can crawl along the floor and you can sneak out the back door. Is there a window open at your house? Maybe you can climb through it and say you were sleep—'

'Or maybe we can open the door and let them think what they like. After all, Janet, we're both consenting adults.'

'I don't understand,' Janet heard her mother say. 'Leesa said they'd both come home late from the hospital but they should be here.'

'Perhaps they went out for breakfast?' It was a male voice who asked the question.

'Dad?' Janet gasped. 'All four of them must be out there.

Oh, my goodness. I'll never live this down. We can't let them find us together. You hide in the bedroom and...' She stopped. 'No. That would look worse. Don't just stand there, Angus. Think!'

'Stop panicking.' Angus reached for her hands and held them in his. 'Just take a deep breath and relax. We'll get through this.'

'Gone out for breakfast?' Mary O'Donnell's voice said. 'My son? Up before the birds? No. They must both be still asleep. Go and knock on Angus's bedroom window, Sean,' she ordered her husband.

'Janet?' Carol Stevenson knocked again.

Angus opened his mouth to reply but Janet's glare stopped him. 'You're right.' She dropped his hands and began edging slowly to the door. 'We're fully clothed. It's all quite innocent, regardless of what they all might think. We've done nothing.'

'Tell me about it,' Angus groaned, and raked a hand through his hair.

She took a shaky breath, before calling, 'Coming, Mum.' Janet opened the door. 'What a...surprise!'

Carol hugged her daughter, before stepping inside the door to admit the others.

'Good morning, angel.' Ron Stevenson enveloped his daughter in a hug and gave her a kiss. 'Thought we'd lost you for a moment.'

'Come on in,' Janet offered.

'Hello, dear,' Mary said as she kissed Janet's cheek. 'Have you seen Angus? We can't raise him no matter how hard we pound on his door.'

Janet gritted her teeth but smiled nonetheless. 'Come in, Mary. He's...um...he's here.'

Mary's eyes widened in surprise before a twinkling of delight shone through. 'Is he indeed? Well, well, well.' She looked over Janet's shoulder. 'Ron, would you mind telling

Sean to stop pounding on Angus's window, otherwise the house might fall down.'

Janet's father did as he'd been told and the two mothers went into the lounge room to say good morning to Angus.

'You're looking lovely as usual,' Angus told his mother as they all sat down.

'Pity I can't say the same for you two. Did you both sleep in your clothes?' The glances between the two older women were ones of suppressed curiosity.

'There was a terrible accident last night,' Janet offered by way of explanation.

'We know. We've already seen Hamish and Leesa.'

'When did you arrive?'

'Yesterday evening. We tried to ring you both but reached your answering machines,' Mary said.

'I couldn't find your mobile phone number,' Carol told Janet, 'so we contacted the hospital when we arrived, only to be told that both Leesa and Hamish were in Theatre. Someone took a message for them and Hamish called Mary early this morning and arranged to meet us for breakfast.'

The two fathers came in and again the greetings were repeated. 'How about putting the kettle on, Janet?' Ron asked his daughter. 'I, for one, could do with a cup of tea.'

'Sure. Sorry. I should have offered. Please, excuse my lack of manners.'

'It's to be expected, dear,' Mary said with a wink. Janet could feel herself begin to blush and quickly left the room.

A few moments later her mother came into the kitchen. 'Need a hand?'

'No.' Janet was setting a tray. 'I've put some muffins into the microwave to defrost.' She stopped fussing for a moment and then looked at her mother. 'You should have told me—uh, I mean us—sooner that you were coming.'

'It was Mary's idea. She wanted to surprise everyone,

and you know what Mary's like when she gets an idea in her head.'

'That stubborn Irish streak still going strong?' Janet asked with a smile, and her mother nodded.

'It seems she was right to want to surprise you. What's going on between you and Angus?'

Janet sighed and looked down at her hands. 'It's all so complicated.'

'You love him.' It was a statement and Janet raised her gaze to meet her mother's, before nodding.

'Then you approve of him?'

'How could I not? I've always viewed both Angus and Hamish as the sons I never had. And to top it all off, I get along famously with his parents.'

Janet gave a brief laugh.

'It's good to see you smile.'

Janet finished getting the tray ready and took the muffins out of the microwave, soft, fluffy and warm.

'Mmm,' Carol said, pinching one off the tray before Janet carried it in. 'You're an excellent cook, my darling.'

'Thanks.' She deposited the tray on the coffee-table and went back for the teapot. Angus followed her.

'Whew! I had to get out of the lions' den. All four parents breathing down my neck.'

'It was your idea to let them in, remember. I wanted you to sneak out and hide.'

'Yes.' A slow smile began to tug at his lips. 'I remember. Well, it's out in the open now.' He reached out a hand to her just as the phone rang. Janet picked it up and glanced at her answering machine whose little red light was flashing four times. If only she'd checked her messages when they'd arrived home last night. Oh, well.

'Dr Stevenson,' she answered.

'Janet, it's Leesa.'

'Hey, sis. Thanks for the warning.'

'I gather the masses have descended on you.'

'Yes.'

'At least we didn't invite you out for breakfast. I thought last night had shaken you up quite a bit and you needed the rest.'

'It did and thank you for being so considerate. However, in hindsight, perhaps waking *us* up and inviting *us* out to breakfast might have been the better option.'

Leesa hadn't missed her sister's clues. 'Angus stayed the night, eh?'

'On the couch. We both fell asleep on the couch.'

'Innocent to the last,' Leesa acknowledged. 'Listen, I have some bad news.'

At the change in her sister's tone Janet sobered and met Angus's gaze. 'What's happened?'

'The John Doe patient you brought in last night—he died fifteen minutes ago. Liver failure.'

'What?' Angus asked, and took the phone from Janet's limp hand. He spoke with Leesa then said goodbye and hung up.

'Leesa and Hamish will be finished at the hospital in an hour and have booked lunch at Giovanni's restaurant in town. They'll meet us there for the big family reunion.'

Janet felt tears prick behind her eyes and Angus enveloped her in a hug. 'It's all right,' he whispered in her ear. 'His blood alcohol reading was quite high. His death is no one's fault but his own.'

'I can't help thinking of everything we went through last night and then he dies. And not only us but everyone else— the ambulance crews, firefighters, police, hospital personnel.' She looked up at him and shook her head. 'This is the reason I chose to be a GP, not a surgeon. I just can't handle this type of situation.'

'I know, and you're an excellent GP—among other

things.' He bent his head and slowly allowed his lips to meet hers.

The kiss was only brief but held so much promise. 'I have some errands to run but I'll pick you up for lunch.'

'Don't worry. I can meet you there or go with my parents.'

'I'll pick you up,' he said with more force.

'All right.' Reluctantly he let her go and she picked up the teapot.

Angus said goodbye to the parents, leaving Janet to ignore their curious glances and wait impatiently for his return.

He was running late. Typical Angus. Janet knew she should have insisted on meeting him at the restaurant but, no, she'd given in to him once more.

She'd dressed in a pair of black trousers teamed with a burgundy top. Her make-up was perfect, as was her hair and jewellery. All she needed now was the man to go with her outfit—Angus.

After checking her appearance in the mirror yet again, she heard a knock at her door. She quickly went to open it, unable to contain her excitement at seeing him again.

'Come on,' he said when she opened the door. 'Sorry I'm late but, hey, you know me.'

'Yes, I do,' Janet said as he helped her on with her coat.

The drive to the Italian restaurant was completed in silence, although Angus did make a point of holding her hand in his while he drove. Janet felt her excitement escalate and intuitively felt the change in his attitude.

When they arrived, the rest of the family were already seated. They ordered and enjoyed a fine feast of Italian food, Janet all the while delighting in the man sitting beside her and holding her hand under the table at every opportunity.

Before they could order dessert, Angus tapped his glass with a spoon and a hush fell over the restaurant. Janet wondered apprehensively what he was up to, and with the change in his attitude she guessed it included herself.

'I'm sorry to bother you all,' he apologised to the patrons, 'but I have something to say.'

A waiter brought him a large, beautifully wrapped parcel, which he handed to Janet. 'Open it.'

Janet reached out a trembling hand, feeling everyone's gaze in the crowded restaurant focused on her. Usually she would meticulously unwrap presents, savouring the enjoyment, but today she couldn't contain herself. She glanced briefly at the rest of her family who all seemed equally surprised at Angus's behaviour.

'It's a coffee-machine,' she said thoughtfully, and a few people at another table laughed. She turned her puzzled gaze to meet Angus's.

'It's for the surgery. If I'm to stay on as your partner, I need *real* coffee.'

'My…' Janet looked at him with astonishment. 'Did you just say…?'

'Partner. Yes. There was a message on my answering machine from the company. Everything's cleared for me to stay. If you'll still have me?'

There wasn't a single sound in the restaurant as they all waited for Janet's answer.

'Uh… Well… Yes.' Janet smiled at him with absolute delight.

Quite a few people started clapping but Angus waved their applause away.

'Janet. I want it all. I know I've told you before but I wasn't quite specific enough. Let me give it another try.'

Angus took Janet's hand in his and actually went down

on one knee. One person wolf-whistled and others clapped. Again, Angus hushed the other patrons.

Janet's heart was pounding so quickly she thought she might go into cardiac arrest, and that would never have done, especially when Angus seemed about to propose.

'Janet, I want to spend our rainy evenings together and enjoy the warmer days when they arrive. I want to enjoy your home cooking, as well as taking you out to dinner. I want to talk with you, laugh with you and just relax with you.'

His gaze seemed to burn into her soul and she licked her suddenly dry lips. 'I want to touch you as you've never been touched before. I want to kiss you as you've never been kissed before. I want to make love to you and hold you until the sun comes up.'

Janet gasped at the thought and blushed. She didn't hear the further clapping from the others and neither did Angus. They had eyes only for each other.

'I want your friendship, I want the attraction between us and I want so much more. Not only do I want all of these things, Janet, I need them and I need them with you. I need marriage. I need children and I need you. Be the permanent fixture in my life, Janet. I love you with all my heart.'

As though on cue, waiters everywhere brought out champagne for all the guests.

'Janet, will you do me the honour of becoming my wife?'

Tears were once again pricking behind her eyes but this time for a very different reason. She bit her lip, before nodding.

'Yes,' she whispered as he enveloped her in a hug. 'I love you,' she said into his ear.

'I know,' he responded. He kissed her lips with a home-coming passion that left Janet completely breathless.

The applause that surrounded them was deafening. A few

people called their congratulations and others whistled.
Everyone in the restaurant received a glass of champagne.

'But where's the engagement ring?' Angus's mother demanded over the noise.

Janet looked into his eyes, which were twinkling with
their usual enjoyment.

'Why don't you take the coffeepot out of the box and
give it a close inspection?' he suggested.

'If you insist,' she replied, feeling a little wary, but did
as he'd suggested.

The glass coffeepot had been filled with bright red rose
petals. Nestled snugly at the top was an exquisite square-
cut ruby with a guard of diamonds on either side.

'Angus!' she breathed with wonder. 'It's... It's... Oh...
It's...' She turned to face him as he took the pot from her
trembling hands. He scooped the ring out and placed it on
the third finger of her left hand. 'You remembered I like
rubies,' she whispered.

'Freesias and rubies, but that's truly *all* I remember.'

Janet looked down at her hand again, the sparkling ruby
and diamonds shining back at her. 'Angus, it's...' she tried
again, but he simply placed a finger over her lips.

'It's stunning, my love. Just like you.'

He kissed her briefly before the rest of the family joined
in, offering their congratulations.

Someone tapped their glass for quiet and Angus and
Janet turned to see Hamish rising to his feet.

'If I may have your attention, I'd like to propose a toast.
To the bride and groom—to be!'

Everyone echoed the toast and drank to their health.

Janet smiled at her fiancée. 'To my groom,' she said as
she sipped from her glass.

'To my bride,' he replied, and kissed her once more.

'And may they live a long life of health and happiness,' Hamish finished for them all.

Look out next month for PARTNERS FOR EVER
and watch Hamish succumb to Leesa.

MILLS & BOON®

Makes any time special™

Mills & Boon publish 29 new titles every month. Select from...

Modern Romance™   Tender Romance™

Sensual Romance™

Medical Romance™   Historical Romance™

MAT2

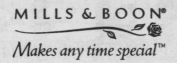

4 FREE
books and a surprise gift!

We would like to take this opportunity to thank you for reading this Mills & Boon® book by offering you the chance to take FOUR more specially selected titles from the Medical Romance™ series absolutely FREE! We're also making this offer to introduce you to the benefits of the Reader Service™—

★ FREE home delivery
★ FREE gifts and competitions
★ FREE monthly Newsletter
★ Exclusive Reader Service discounts
★ Books available before they're in the shops

Accepting these FREE books and gift places you under no obligation to buy, you may cancel at any time, even after receiving your free shipment. Simply complete your details below and return the entire page to the address below. *You don't even need a stamp!*

YES! Please send me 4 free Medical Romance books and a surprise gift. I understand that unless you hear from me, I will receive 6 superb new titles every month for just £2.40 each, postage and packing free. I am under no obligation to purchase any books and may cancel my subscription at any time. The free books and gift will be mine to keep in any case.

M0ZEA

Ms/Mrs/Miss/Mr ....Initials.................................
BLOCK CAPITALS PLEASE
Surname ....
Address ....

....

....Postcode................................

Send this whole page to:
UK: FREEPOST CN81, Croydon, CR9 3WZ
EIRE: PO Box 4546, Kilcock, County Kildare (stamp required)